BEWARE THE BOOGERMAN

A Cold Shivers Nightmare

By
D Glenn Casey

www.DGlennCasey.com

The novel, *Beware The Boogerman* is a work of fiction. Names, characters, places, and incidents either are the product of the author's imagination or are used fictitiously. Any resemblance to actual persons, living or dead, events, or locales is entirely coincidental.

Copyright © 2018 by D Glenn Casey

All rights reserved. No part of this publication may be reproduced, stored in a retrieval system or transmitted in any form or by any means, electronic, mechanical, recording or otherwise, without the prior written permission of the author.

Cover design: D Glenn Casey

Printed in the United States of America

ISBN: 978-1-9830246-5-8

Other works by D Glenn Casey
(All available in Kindle Unlimited and as paperbacks)

The Chronicles of Wyndweir
The Tales of Garlan ~ Prequel
Wicked Rising ~ Book One
The Wrath ~ Book Two

A Cold Shivers Nightmares
Beware The Boogerman
Shattered Prisons

Other full-length novels
Into The Wishing Well

Table of Contents ~ Beware The Boogerman

Prologue - Prattville Sheriff's Department..............1
Chapter 1 - Buster on the Loose................................7
Chapter 2 - Where it all began.................................23
Chapter 3 - Return of the Boogerman...................32
Chapter 4 - Face to face with terror.......................48
Chapter 5 - Meeting a new ally...............................65
Chapter 6 - Date night with a side of beating.......83
Chapter 7 - There is no escape..............................104
Chapter 8 - No more pumpkin muffins...............117
Chapter 9 - Hospitals are for the dying...............122
Chapter 10 - Missing mom......................................131
Chapter 11 - Getting a better idea.........................149
Chapter 12 - Even the ogres trembled..................157
Chapter 13 - The hook is set...................................177
Chapter 14 - The hunt begins................................190
Chapter 15 - The battle for it all............................207
Chapter 16 - In the clutches of the demon...........220
Chapter 17 - It all makes sense now.....................233
Chapter 18 - The final battle..................................250
Chapter 19 - Another day in Monster Town.......262

BEWARE THE BOOGERMAN

A Cold Shivers Nightmare

BY
D Glenn Casey

Prologue
~~
Prattville Sheriff's Department

Prattville, Nebraska. Right in the heart of the good ol' USA. Or as some have come to call it, Prattvile. It's usually the kids that call it that. The grown-ups like their quiet, little town just the way it is. Peaceful, clean and beautiful. No other town like it within a hundred miles.

There is one other name that Prattville is known by, but the residents would prefer it not get around, so please keep it a secret. The last thing the good people of Prattville want are hordes of people coming to their town and poking their noses where they don't belong. Things like that tend to end badly for the Prattville residents and for those that come to town looking for something else.

The other name by which Prattville is known is Monster Town. But, you didn't hear that here. Please keep it between us and under no circumstances should you post this information to Facebook or Twitter or Instagram or any of those other ridiculous websites that think they have a good bead about how the world works. They don't know squat.

Prattville came by the nickname of Monster Town because of rumors that there are monsters living there. Why else would it be called Monster Town? Because it's full of bunny rabbits? If it were full of bunny rabbits it would be called Bunny Rabbit Town. If it were full of aliens it would be called Alien Town.

However, a case could be made that some of the monsters are probably from out of town. Way out of town.

Ask any of the residents in town about the so-called monsters that live there and they will give you a look that says, *"Oh boy, here's another one of those crazy monster hunters."* And then they will tell you that there are no such thing as monsters and try to sell you a t-shirt that says you spent three days in Monster Town and all you got was this crappy t-shirt. The guy that designs the t-shirts is now rich from all the shirts sold.

If you drive down the main street through Prattville, it looks like any other small town in the heart of the country. A small general store, a farmer's supply store, a John Deere tractor dealership and a couple of convenience stores and gas stations that the residents hope you will use to get the hell out of town.

There is even a beauty parlor where the women of the town sit under those giant glass bubbles to get their hair dried. When was the last time you saw a real beauty parlor? There is a rumor going around that when the women sit under the hair dryers, they are actually having their brains recharged, but that is just a rumor. You didn't hear that here either.

Another building you will see on the main drag is the Sheriff's Department, usually with a couple of sheriff's vehicles outside. It is a one story, brick building, but it's said there is a secret basement for detaining monsters, but that's also just a rumor. Don't go looking for the secret basement because it doesn't exist. Probably. Maybe.

So, what do the sheriff and his deputies do all day long in this quiet little town? Not much, they will tell you. That's why there are only three of them in the whole department. The most excitement they will tell you about is when Farmer Taylor's hogs got loose in Farmer Smith's watermelon patch and set about destroying the nearly ripened watermelons. Farmer Smith came out of his house with a shotgun and was ready to turn all those hogs into bacon, but the sheriff and one of his deputies showed up and calmed things down. A little.

It took a good hour to get the hogs back on their own side of the fence. You ever try to get a hog to stop eating watermelons and go back to where it came from? It is not as easy as you've been led to believe.

Farmer Taylor got a bill from Farmer Smith for all the lost watermelons and the judge told him to pay it or Farmer Smith could take a half a dozen of his hogs to the butcher and fill his freezer with pork chops and sausage. Farmer Taylor paid the bill.

And the sheriff will tell you that is the most exciting thing that's happened in Prattville in the last few years. You better believe him because he is an officer of the law and he wouldn't lie to you. He has been the sheriff of Prattville since forever. Nobody knows how long he's been the sheriff because nobody can remember a time when he wasn't the sheriff.

His job is usually up for election every four years, but no one has ever run against him in the election because everyone is quite happy with the way he's doing things. He keeps things nice and peaceful in Prattville and that's the way the residents like it.

His name is John Dinkendorfer and his name badge says *John*. Just *John*. Dinkendorfer would be way too long to put on the name badge. Plus, he got tired of all the giggles from people when he'd stop them for speeding through his town. So, call him Sheriff John or just Sheriff.

His number one deputy is also the one that gives him the most trouble. That's because he is actually a she and her last name is also Dinkendorfer and she is Sheriff John's daughter, Debbie Dinkendorfer.

Rumor has it that some brave souls have called her Deputy Dinkie, but woe be unto the person who called her that if they are not a really good friend. She has been known to lock people up for that. Some have tried to say they were locked up for three days in the secret basement jail cells, but those don't exist, remember? So don't believe anyone that tells you that. Especially when they start to rant about how they were stuck in the middle cell with a large, rabid werewolf on one side and a giant, slimy who-the-hell-knows-what on the other side. Just tell them to stop smoking that funny stuff and their nightmares should end.

Deputy Dinkie, err, umm, Deputy Dinkendorfer stands at about five and a half feet tall and weighs about one hundred and twenty-five pounds. She only weighs that after she puts on her belt with her gun and night stick and taser. And her heavy boots.

Some would say she is too skinny and couldn't possibly be a good sheriff's deputy, but they have never seen her take down a man a foot taller than her and weighing twice as much as her.

She did that to Billy Ray Hanson one night, but some will tell you it was because Billy Ray was really drunk and he fell down. But, that doesn't explain why, whenever Billy Ray sees the deputy walking down the street, he always crosses the street, to the other side. Maybe it's just because he isn't very friendly.

The other deputy, the one that works the night shift is Cal Worhl. He's been a deputy now for about six years, since getting out of the army, where he was a military policeman. He grew up near Chicago and decided he'd had enough of the big city life and wanted something a little slower. A friend of his told him about Prattville and that they needed a deputy sheriff. He came to town and talked to Sheriff John and was a deputy one week later. He likes his quiet life, with his small piece of land just outside of town.

And last, but certainly not least, is Mabel. She is the heart and soul of the sheriff's department and everyone knows it. She handles everything in the office, from booking ne'er-do-wells to manning the phones and radio. When she's not in church on Sunday, singing in the choir, she can be found in the office, running a tight ship and expecting everyone to toe the line.

So that is the sheriff's department in Prattville. Four brave men and women that look after the safety and well-being of the good folks that call Prattville home.

And they will tell you that there are no such thing as monsters.

Chapter 1

~~

Buster on the Loose

It was a beautiful day. The sun was shining, but it wasn't hot at all. The air was clean and everything felt right with the world.

"Sheriff John?"

The sheriff snapped out of his daydream and grabbed the radio, almost spilling his cup of coffee in his lap.

"Yes, Mabel. What's up?"

"Kyle Manning called and said Buster is loose again. I'd send Cal, but he's already left for the day."

"How about Debbie? Is she in yet?"

"Not yet, sheriff. Looks like it's up to you today."

Sheriff John leaned forward and banged his forehead on his steering wheel a couple of times. For some reason, it felt a whole lot better than to go chasing after some dog that got loose.

Oh, good grief.

If there was one thing he didn't want to do after a nice, peaceful weekend, was to go chasing after Buster, just because Kyle Manning couldn't keep him on the property. Sitting out here, just off Highway 263, under the shade of the large oak tree near Carl Simpkin's farm was about as much excitement as he wanted today. All he wanted to do was listen to his audiobook library of Jack Reacher novels.

That Jack Reacher. What a life. Nowhere to be, no one to answer to and he got to be judge, jury and executioner when the situation warranted it. What he wouldn't give to be Jack Reacher at that moment.

"Sheriff?"

"I'm on my way, Mabel."

He reached down and turned the key in the ignition. The sound of 425 horses under the hood coming to life always brought a smile to his face. The occasional speeder that came through town didn't stand a chance. One thing he liked about this small town is they made sure he had the right tools for the job. This brand new Chevy Blazer, with all the cop car equipment was just such a tool.

He slipped the Blazer into gear and rolled onto the highway and headed toward the other side of town. The Manning farm was just past the city limits, down by the creek.

Rolling through town, he looked at the department and noticed Debbie's Blazer wasn't there. It wasn't like her to be late on a Monday morning and if she didn't turn up by the time he got finished with Buster, he'd swing by her place to check on her.

She had inherited his old, hand-me-down cruiser because rank has its privileges. Not that it was a bad truck. It was still in good condition and ran great. Earl at the garage made sure all the vehicles were in tip-top condition.

The sheriff waved at a few residents that were out and about, as he made his way across town. As he drove over a small rise in the road and looked down the other side, he could see the glistening water of the creek about a mile away and the Manning farm was just this side of the bridge.

Kyle was standing out by the end of his driveway, waiting for him. As he reached the bottom of the long hill, he switched on his lights and pulled over. Not that there was any traffic to worry about. He just liked looking official with his lights on.

He pushed the button on his armrest and the window on the passenger side rolled down and Kyle leaned down.

"Good morning sheriff. How's things today?"

"Well, I don't know, Kyle. Suppose you tell me."

Kyle took a deep breath, not wanting to have to say it, but it needed to be said.

"He got out again. I know, I know. You said if he got out again there'd be trouble. And we really tried to keep him in, but … well, you know how he gets when the full moon approaches."

Sheriff John dropped his head and closed his eyes. He shook his head, wondering if the rest of the week was going to be like this.

"Alright, where did he go? Down along the creek

again?"

Kyle didn't say anything at first and the sheriff looked up at him.

"Kyle?"

Kyle took another deep breath and then said, "No, sheriff, he cut right out the gate and headed across the bridge."

"What?!" yelled the sheriff. "You're telling me he's heading toward Hobart?!"

Kyle nodded slowly and then jumped back as the sheriff jammed his foot down on the gas and the Blazer shot back onto the pavement, spraying rocks and dirt all over the place.

He grabbed his radio and keyed the mic, "Debbie, you out there?"

A couple of seconds later he heard her voice.

"Yes, daddy, I'm here."

"That's sheriff to you, young lady. And just exactly where is here?"

"I'm at Earl's. The Blazer is running a little rough and he's fiddling with it. What's up?"

"Well, tell him to stop fiddling and get your tail on the road! Buster got loose again and this time he's headed towards Hobart!"

Debbie jumped up out of the chair in Earl's back office like she had been shot out of a cannon. She had been reading one of his two year old Soldier of

Fortune magazines, checking to see if there were any new weapons she needed to know about.

"Oh good lord!" she yelled as she ran to her truck. "Close it up, Earl! We got an emergency!"

Earl got out from under the hood and reached up and pulled it down.

"Buster got loose again, huh?"

"Yeah, and he's heading for Hobart."

"Well, that'll wake up that sleepy, little town."

Debbie started the engine and revved it up a couple of times.

She leaned out the window, looked at Earl and yelled, "This is not a joking matter, Earl!"

Earl just laughed and said, "It will be later tonight at the saloon when you tell us all about it."

Debbie shook her head and slammed the truck into reverse, squealing her tires backing out onto the highway. Earl just laughed and waved goodbye.

Dropping into Drive, she reached over and flipped on the lights and siren and tore through town like a bat out of whatever. It wasn't very often she got to run full lights and siren, but this kind of emergency was something that warranted it.

The quiet, little town of Prattville was just beginning to come to life this morning and there were a few people out, some walking along the sidewalk and others doing their damnedest to get the hell out of the way of the deputy's vehicle.

In less than a minute she flew over the crest of the hill heading toward the creek. And *flew over* is the right phrase, because the Blazer's tires were at least a foot off the ground.

Kyle waved at her as she rocketed past.

She didn't have time to wave back. It was also due to the fact that she didn't want to take her hands off the wheel as she wrestled for control of the screaming beast.

She could hear her daddy on the radio with Mabel at the department.

"Mabel, I need you to get on the phone with Chief Handley in Hobart and tell him he has a code red coming his way, down Highway 2. Will probably hit his town in less than an hour!"

"I'm dialing as we speak."

After a few minutes, Debbie could see her dad's truck about a mile ahead and she gunned her engine to catch up with him. As she passed mile marker 228 she realized that they had less than ninety miles to catch Buster and stop him before he reached Hobart and put a fright into those people the likes of which they'd never had.

A couple of miles later she caught and blew right past her dad. Sheriff John had to take his eyes off the road for a second to look down and see how fast he was going. His speedometer showed he was cruising along at a leisurely 138 miles per hour.

"Debbie! You're going to get yourself killed!" the sheriff yelled into his radio.

"We have to stop him, sheriff!"

"I know that. Don't you think I know that, young lady?"

"All I know is that you said you'd blast him into nothingness the next time he got out. I'm trying to stop that."

Sheriff John pressed his gas pedal down even harder, but it was no use. His 425 horses were never going to keep up with her 650 and her penchant for driving like a race car driver.

He was going to have to speak to Earl about making his truck faster or making hers slower.

Debbie looked way out in the distance and she could see a dark spot moving along the highway at a very high rate of speed. No matter how fast Buster was, he couldn't outrun her and her truck.

Gotcha you mangy mutt.

She glanced in her rear view mirror and saw that her dad was already about a half a mile back and quickly falling further behind. She was going to need all the room between them she could get.

In a few more miles she caught up to the dog, who was running along at a speed of at least seventy miles an hour. She slowed her Blazer and rolled down her window as she came up alongside him.

"Buster! You better stop right now and get in this

truck!"

The big, black dog looked at her with fire in his eyes and foam coming from his mouth. He was just barely breathing hard. He was almost as big as her Blazer and she could feel the pounding of his paws on the pavement, even as she was racing along beside him.

"Don't test me, you dumb dog!" she yelled at him. "Daddy is right behind us and he is ready to vaporize you!"

Buster looked at her with evil in his eyes and growled at her.

"Oh, you did NOT growl at me! Alright you spawn of the devil, if that's the way you want to play it!"

Debbie looked forward again and in the distance, could see the lights of three police cars from Hobart. They were about six miles away on this straight as an arrow road and lined up across both lanes. Even though they were too far away to see, Debbie knew their officers were probably cowering behind their cars, getting ready to unleash all the fury of Hell on this beast coming down the road. She knew she couldn't let that happen. Mostly because she knew their weapons wouldn't make a bit of difference.

She called on her engine again and started pulling away from Buster.

When she was only about a hundred yards away

from the police cars, she slammed on the brakes, yanked the emergency brake and cranked the steering wheel. Her Blazer went into a power slide, leaving four perfect skid marks down the road. The Blazer came to a stop just twenty feet from the police cars and she bailed out of the driver's seat before the truck had even settled.

As she ran around to the back of the Blazer, she looked at the Hobart officers and saw a bit of terror in the eyes of two of them. The two officers were about ready to shoot at anything that moved. Chief Handley was just standing behind them and he smiled at her, while he enjoyed his morning cup of coffee.

"Mornin' boys," she said with a big smile, as she yanked open the back door of her Blazer. She leaned in and lifted a lid in the floor and revealed a security code panel. She punched in her ten digit code and the floor in the back of the Blazer lifted up to reveal a great number of weapons. She reached in and pulled out one that looked an awful lot like a bazooka.

Hoisting it onto her shoulder, she walked back to the front of her Blazer and looked down the road. She could see Buster still coming and her dad was right behind him. If she knew her daddy, he was probably getting ready to shoot Buster right from the front seat of his truck. She couldn't let that happen.

As she started looking through the sight, she felt someone walk up beside her.

15

"Mornin', deputy."

Without taking her eyes away from the sight, she said, "Mornin', Chief Handley. How's that boy of yours today?"

"Oh, you know. Same ol', same ol'. Every day is about the same. How about you?"

Debbie twisted a dial on the side of the sight and Buster came into focus. She could see the foam in his mouth and the red in his eyes.

"I know what you mean." said Debbie, as she brought the cross-hairs right onto the chest of the charging beast.

"Hey, Cindy is wondering if you're ever going to call her," said the chief. "After you two graduated from high school, she just doesn't hear from you anymore."

Buster was now less than a mile away and the sheriff was closing the gap fast.

"I know and I'm really sorry about that. I didn't realize being a deputy was going to take so much of my time. But, I promise I'll call her in the next day or so."

"That would be great."

The chief looked down the road, taking another sip of his coffee and could see the charging mutt. He wasn't too worried about it, but he knew his two officers behind him were probably getting very nervous.

Then, the bazooka erupted and a ball of light screamed away, toward the snarling dog. But, this dog weren't no fool. He juked just as the bazooka fired and the ball of light flew right past him and slammed into the sheriff's truck.

Sheriff John saw the ball of light heading right at him, but he had nowhere to go and cringed as the blast hit the front of the truck head on. In less than one second, the charge from the ball of energy burned out every wire in his truck and he was without power.

"Darn it! Daddy's gonna be mad. His brand new truck, too."

She aimed and fired again, but the dog jumped as she fired, sailing right over the blast and kept on coming. Debbie decided she had had enough of this crap and she flipped a locking switch on the bazooka and yanked on the pistol grip. It came away from the tube of the bazooka and with it, came a smaller barrel. Now Debbie held a pistol with a long, glass barrel. It glowed with a bright, blue light. She tossed the bazooka tube over her shoulder and the chief snatched it out of the air without any trouble.

Debbie started firing as the dog got closer. When Buster was only about fifty feet away, he launched himself into the air, right at Debbie, with teeth bared and snarling like he wanted to rip her to pieces.

Boom!

One last shot from the pistol and it caught Buster right in the chest. He crashed to the pavement and shook the earth around them. His body skidded to a stop up against the sole of Debbie's boot. Only his body wasn't huge anymore.

He was just a little wiener dog and he was out cold.

Debbie knelt down on one knee and stroked his head.

"Buster, one of these days."

As she stood up, Sheriff John came walking up with a nasty looking pistol of his own.

"Don't you be shooting Buster, daddy."

"I'm not going to shoot him. I'm going to shoot you! Look what you did to my truck!"

"Sorry," she said as she looked back at the smoking truck, crippled on the side of the road.

"Sorry? Sorry! It's a brand new truck!"

"Well, it still is."

The chief stepped up and held out his hand, "Mornin', Sheriff John."

The sheriff was still seeing red, but he went to hold out his hand to the chief, but the chief pulled his hand away.

"No, sheriff, I want you to hand me your gun so you don't shoot your daughter."

The sheriff shook his head and then brought the pistol up and banged it into his forehead a couple of times. He turned back around and looked at his truck.

"Aghhh!" yelled the sheriff as he shoved his weapon back into his holster.

The two other police officers came slowly walking around the Blazer, still with their guns drawn, looking like they were ready to face the devil himself.

"Where's that big dog?" asked one of them.

"What big dog?" asked the chief.

The officer stepped around Debbie and looked down and the only thing he saw was a little wiener dog, laying on the ground, pawing and snarling in its sleep.

"I know what I saw, chief. It was huge and it was rabid."

"You been drinking again, Officer Jeffers?"

"Uhh, no sir."

"Okay." said the chief, "Hey, why don't you two head on back to town and I'll finish this up."

As the two of them walked back to their cars, they glanced into the back of Debbie's Blazer. The assortment of guns was staggering, some of which neither one of them had ever seen before. A lot of them were glowing, like they were powered by something that was not gunpowder.

Debbie turned to the chief and said, "Sorry about all the excitement today, chief."

"Hey, that's okay. We generally don't get much excitement over here in Hobart."

"Well, you could come over to Prattville once in a while and see how we do things." said Debbie with a smile.

"Over to Monster Town? I don't think so."

"Come on, chief. It'd be fun."

"That kind of fun I just don't need in my life."

Debbie laughed and then walked around to the back of her truck and put her weapon away and then lowered the floor and secured the weapons vault.

Then she grabbed a small cage that was behind the seat and walked around to where Buster was still laying on the ground. She knelt down and picked him up, as he snapped and growled in his sleep. She put him in the cage and closed it, flipping an electrical switch on top. There was an energy field that would keep Buster from growing if he were to wake up. Then she picked him up and carried him back and put it in the Blazer and closed the back door.

As she was walking back to the front she could see her daddy was standing off a little ways, just looking back at his smoking truck and she felt a little sorry for him. She pulled out her phone and dialed a number and waited.

"Earl, hey, this is Debbie. Yeah, could you please bring your flatbed out here to Highway 2 about ten miles east of Hobart and pick up daddy's truck? Yeah, it's suffered little damage and you're going to need to repair it. Thanks."

She stopped next to the chief as he was looking at her dad wondering what he could say to help calm him down.

"He really loves that truck," said Debbie.

"He'll get over it. Earl will fix it like brand-new and he'll be right back on the road."

The chief looked around and then back at his quiet, little town, happy that its solitude had been preserved for one more day.

"Well, if we're all done here, I'll go ahead and take off. Don't forget to call Cindy. She'd love to hear from you."

"I'll do that, chief," said Debbie.

The chief patted her on the shoulder, then turned and walked back toward his car. Debbie walked over to her dad and put her arm around his waist and squeezed a little.

"Sorry about your truck, daddy."

"I was just getting it broke in.

"Well, Earl is on his way and he'll take it back to the shop and in a couple of days you'll have a brand new truck again."

Sheriff John let out a big sigh as he continued to look at the truck, just smoking on the side of the road. It looked just like those trucks you see in the news, bombed out and wrecked in some war halfway around the world.

"Let's head back to Manning's farm." said Debbie.

"Now there's somebody you can yell at that deserves it."

They climbed into Debbie's Blazer and she turned and headed back towards Prattville. About halfway back they saw Earl driving towards Hobart in the tow truck and Debbie waved at him as they went by.

Just another day in Monster Town.

Chapter 2

~~

Where it all began

Chasing down Buster was the most exciting part of the day for the deputy and sheriff. It was a lot more excitement than Sheriff John wanted to see on a daily basis.

Every time he thought about that demon dog, he would get the shakes. Not because Buster scared him. Nope, that wasn't it at all. It was because it was everything he could do not to go down the Manning place and scatter his atoms all over the universe.

About the middle of the afternoon, Sheriff John walked out the door of the department and headed down the street to Earl's garage. When he got there, he just stood in the open door of the garage bay and just stared at his crippled Blazer. He didn't know whether to laugh or cry.

"Well, sheriff, looks like you did a number on it this time."

The sheriff turned and looked at a smiling Earl. The sheriff gave him a look that wiped that smile right off his face.

"I didn't do it! Debbie did it to me!"

"Weeeellllll, I'm purdy sure she didn't do it on purpose. Oh, I found something."

Earl walked over and opened the passenger door and reached in. When he came back out of the garage he was holding the sheriff's mp3 player and the wires to the earbuds looked a little extra crispy.

"Oh no," said the sheriff as he took the player from Earl.

He pressed the power button and got nothing. He held the power button down for a few seconds and then the unit powered up. He breathed a sigh of relief until he checked the library of audiobooks. It was completely empty. It had been wiped clean by the blast from Debbie's bazooka. All of his Jack Reacher audiobooks were gone.

"Aghh!" he yelled as he fought every impulse to throw the player as far as he could.

He was going to make her pay, even if she was his daughter.

"What's the matter sheriff? It's not working?"

He took a deep breath and then remembered that he had all the audiobooks backed up on the computer at home, so all he needed to do was hook the player up and transfer them back. He stuffed the player into his pocket and turned around.

"No, no. It's working fine. I'm just a little frustrated at seeing my new truck coming back to town on the back of your tow truck."

"Not to worry, sheriff. I'll have it up and running again in a couple of days."

As the sheriff turned to walk out the door of the garage, he turned back and asked, "Hey Earl, is there any way you can slow Debbie's truck down?"

~~~~

Debbie sat in the rocking chair on her front porch and looked out at the fields that stretched away from her place. Her little house sat just west of Farmer Smith's patch of ground and her front porch faced to the west, giving her great views of the sunsets in the evening. She was happy she didn't live on the other side, next to Farmer Taylor's hog pen and have to smell them stinky pigs. Of course, she did catch a whiff of them every now and then when the breeze shifted directions.

She rocked back and forth and took a sip of her soda. She almost giggled when she thought about the events of that morning. She didn't really mean to blast her daddy's truck.

She had to make sure she was out in front of the office when Cal came into work, to warn him not to smile or laugh when he heard about the wire-frying incident.

Then she felt sorry for Kyle Manning. The sheriff sure laid into him when they got Buster back to his cage. The sheriff kept wanting to take the small cage with Buster in it down to the creek and toss it in, but

Debbie stood her ground and wouldn't let him do it.

Buster was just a sweet, little, wiener dog that turned into a monster hound as they got closer to the full moon each month. He wasn't a werewolf. He was a demon dog and the full moon was the trigger that set off his change each month.

Usually, Kyle was able to keep him locked up for those few days. He had a special cage built in his barn that was big and strong enough to hold Buster. But, about once a year, that demon dog would get loose and take off and it was the sheriff department's job to track him down and subdue him.

As she sat and enjoyed the evening breeze, without the smell of the hogs that evening, she started thinking back to when she first realized this little town was different.

She was just a little girl, in the third grade and one day her best friend, Cindy, disappeared from the playground. She didn't see it happen and no one else did either, but some of the kids started saying it was the Boogerman that got her.

That's when she realized she could punch someone right in the nose to get her point across. Kenny Kline started going on about how Cindy was taken by the Boogerman because he was hungry and was going to eat her for dinner. When Debbie demanded that he stop saying that, Kenny just laughed in her face. He was dancing around, chanting, "The Boogerman gonna eat her, the Boogerman gonna eat her."

Next thing he knew, he was laying on the ground with his nose rearranged across his face and blood running down over his mouth. Debbie was standing over him and telling him that if he didn't stop, she was going to make sure to trade him to the Boogerman and get Cindy back.

About that time, one of the teachers finally arrived at the scene of the crime and hauled Debbie to the principal's office. Her dad was called and she had to sit there and wait. Sitting there with a scowl on her face, ready to fight anyone that looked at her funny.

Back then, she was the tiniest, skinniest kid in the third grade, but also the toughest. It was probably because she was so small that she became so tough. When you're the little kid and the big kids think they can pick on you, you learn to fight and defend yourself real quick.

When her daddy showed up, he put on a good show, saying that hitting Kenny was wrong and she was going to be punished when they got home. Her dad had only been the sheriff for about two years when this happened and the townsfolk were already starting to like him.

She did get punished when she got home. She was punished with a bowl of ice cream, a wink from her daddy, telling her he was proud of her for not backing down from Kenny and then they curled up on the couch and watched a monster movie together.

Kenny Kline never bothered her again.

The next day Cindy was found, locked in a cage in an abandoned barn a couple of miles north of town. She was scared, but uneaten. She said the man who took her had red eyes, long fingernails and his breath stunk like a werewolf's. Debbie always wondered how Cindy would know what a werewolf's breath smelled like, but she never really asked.

A lot of people wrote off her description as just the story of a scared little girl. Sheriff John knew better and he and his deputies started scouring the area, looking for the demon, but they never found him.

Debbie believed Cindy and told her so. It was almost a year before her friend could sleep with the lights off, even when they had sleep overs.

Most towns would have called this monster the Boogieman, but the little kids mispronounced its name and it stuck.

But, the Boogerman wasn't finished. After Cindy was found, it was if he went on a rampage, mad because he had lost his prize. Over the course of a couple of weeks, five monsters were killed and beheaded.

The sheriff and his deputies did everything they

could to find out who this Boogerman was and stop the killings, but in the end, they just stopped all by themselves. No one ever knew why.

And five monster heads were never found.

The rampage was a little too much for a couple of the deputies and they decided to find employment elsewhere. Elsewhere being any place a long ways away from Monster Town. That just left the sheriff and one deputy. His name was Dean Cartwright.

One day, when she was about twelve, Debbie asked her dad about the rumor there were monsters living in Prattville and he sat her down and told her she didn't need to worry. He told her most of the monsters were just people that wanted to live peacefully and just be left alone. Every now and then there was one that would start to act up and it became his job to stop them.

"Yes, Debbie," he said, looking her straight in the eyes, "monsters do exist and they live here in Prattville."

He laughed when her only response was, "Cool!"

She and Cindy stayed friends all through school. Then she went into the military and Cindy ended up getting married to Bart Handley, who is now the Chief of Police in Hobart. They hadn't talked in quite awhile and Debbie felt really bad about that. She already planned to call her the next morning and maybe drive over to Hobart and have lunch with her.

While she was in the military, Debbie became a military police officer and earned a reputation of being tough as nails.

While in the army, she met a guy named Cal Worhl and she told him about Prattville and how her dad was the sheriff. She left out the part about monsters.

When Cal was getting ready to separate from the army, Debbie told him he should go talk to her dad about a job.

She told him it would never be boring.

Two years later when she got out of the army, she came home and marched right into her daddy's office and said she wanted a job as one of his deputies. At first, he didn't like the idea, but he was never able to turn her down when she really wanted something and he knew she would be perfect for the job. She already had all the training she needed thanks to the U. S. Army.

That was four years ago and her life had never been boring since.

Buying the little house on ten acres just outside the town limits was paradise to her, allowing her to spend the evenings sitting on the front porch, sometimes reading and sometimes just cleaning her weapons. Depended on what her mood was from the day. Tonight, it was just relaxing with a cold Coke, listening to the night critters chirping and buzzing.

~~~~

Later that night, when the world had gone to sleep, there was a scream that shattered the quiet of the witching hour. It was a scream that would have caused the blood to run cold in the putrid, old veins of the devil, himself.

The birds in the trees took to the air in fright, some even dying of heart attacks before they flew ten feet. But, the birds and some chickens in Farmer Smith's coops were the only ones to hear the scream. Oh, and the hogs on Farmer Taylor's farm. They stopped rooting around in the mud and crammed themselves into their shelter, all huddled up in one corner.

Old lady Jensen lived about two miles outside of town, on a little piece of land with a small country home. It was just a mile or so the other side of Taylor's farm. Ever since her husband had passed away, she had almost become a recluse. They would see her in town about once a month to buy some groceries that she couldn't grow in her garden, but that was about it. Other than that, nobody ever saw much of her.

After tonight, no one would ever see her in town again.

Chapter 3

~~

Return of the Boogerman

Sheriff John looked up from his desk when he heard the front door of the office open. It was Terry, the old guy that ran the small, country store across the street. His wife, Milly, could make pumpkin muffins like nobody's business.

"Hey sheriff."

"Terry, how you doin' today?"

"I'm doing pretty good. Hey, the reason I come over is because Clara Jensen didn't come into town this week for her usual supplies. She would have gotten her government check on Monday and I would have expected to see that rattle-trap truck of hers that day or on Tuesday."

Sheriff John sat back in his chair and looked at Terry. He took a deep breath and nodded.

"I guess we should send someone out there to check up on her."

"Probably wouldn't hurt."

"Okay, thanks Terry."

"You betcha. Take it easy, sheriff."

As Terry turned and headed back out the door, Sheriff John leaned over and pressed the talk button on the radio.

"Debbie, you out there?"

"Yeah, sheriff. What's up?"

"I need you to do a welfare check. Drive on out to Clara Jensen's place and just make sure she's okay."

"Will do, sheriff."

A couple of minutes later, Mabel came through the front door.

"Good mornin', Mabel."

"Morning to you, too, sheriff. Anything exciting I should know about."

"In this town? Not hardly."

Mabel laughed, "That's the same thing you said the last time Buster got out."

The sheriff just hung his head and thought seriously of banging it on the desk a couple of times.

"Don't remind me. It took Earl three days to get my truck running right after Debbie blasted it."

"Yes he did, but it also gave you a chance to ride around with your daughter for three days, spending some much needed time with her."

Looking at his gal Friday, he clenched his jaws, wondering if he should say what he really thought.

Mabel got herself a cup of coffee and sat down at her desk. She started going through the paperwork, checking to see what needed to be done for the day.

About twenty minutes later the radio came to life.

"Sheriff?"

"Yeah, Debbie, what's the story?"

"I think you should come out here."

"Do I really have to? You know Clara don't like me much."

"Daddy, please come out here."

Even Mabel perked at the word *daddy*. Something was terribly wrong for Debbie to say that over the radio. They could both hear the shakiness in her voice. Sheriff John looked at Mabel and then stood up. He leaned over and pressed the Talk button again.

"Sit tight. I'm on my way."

Grabbing his hat and keys, he headed out to his truck. He pointed it east and barely touched his brakes at the two stop signs before hitting the open stretch of highway to the Jensen place.

He crested a small hill and could see the house, sitting about a hundred yards back from the road and he saw Debbie's truck sitting out front. As he got closer to the driveway, he could see she was sitting in the front seat of her truck and as he pulled up behind her, she didn't move at all.

He got out of his truck and walked to her driver's door and saw she was just sitting there, staring at the house, trying to control her breathing.

"What's up, kiddo?"

She turned and looked at him and he could see she was on the verge of losing it.

"It's bad, daddy. It's really bad."

She turned and looked back at the house, but

made no move to exit the truck, or go into the house with him.

He looked at the house and could see the front door was open. He patted Debbie on the shoulder and said, "You just stay here."

As he walked to the steps leading to the porch, he felt the urge to draw his gun, but if Debbie wasn't drawing hers, he probably didn't need to either.

He drew it anyway.

As he stepped to the door, he could smell it. He knew exactly what he was dealing with here. A dead body that's been laying around for a few days in this heat is going to smell mighty ripe. This one had obviously passed its expiration date.

He pulled the screen door open and stepped inside. It was immediately obvious there had been some sort of attack. There was dried blood on the walls of the living room and a huge spot of blood on the floor, near the kitchen door. Furniture was turned over and lots of froufrou nick-knacks were busted all over the place.

As he walked across the living room, he could feel the dried blood crunching under his feet and as he got closer to the kitchen door, he saw that there was a wide trail of blood across the linoleum floor, as if a body had been dragged.

He was thinking that he had seen the worst of it, but he was wrong. As he followed the trail across the kitchen he came to the back door. There was a doggy door near the bottom and there was blood and skin all around the opening, as if the body had been pulled through the door, but it was too big for the opening.

He looked and noticed the door was still locked, so no one had come through the door. He unlocked the door, opened it and stepped out onto the back porch. There was some blood across the porch, but because of the rain over the past couple of days, most of it had been washed away. He could see the blood trailed off toward the wooded hillside about a hundred yards behind the house.

As he stood and looked at the trees, a wave of cold shivers washed over his body. He knew he wasn't dealing with a simple murder of a little old lady. This was something a little more scary.

He reached up and keyed the mic on his shoulder.

"Mabel?"

"Go ahead, sheriff."

"I need you to get in touch with Bill Bennett and have have him bring his hounds to the Jensen place."

"Will do sheriff. Is it that bad?"

"Yes, Mabel, I'm afraid it is."

He stepped down off the porch and looked back at the trees. He knew he needed to investigate, but there was no way in hell he was going out there alone.

He turned and walked around the house and

back to the front driveway. Debbie had gotten herself composed and was standing outside her truck, leaning up against the front fender.

"I don't like it, daddy."

"I don't like it either, punkin. This has all the makings of being a monster on monster killing and that's the last thing we need."

"But Clara was just a sweet old lady. She just wanted to live out the rest of her days in peace and be left alone."

"Yes, she was, but she was also a monster."

"An old monster. When was the last time she changed into a gargoyle? It's been years and even then, she could hardly move with all the arthritis and old age in her body."

Sheriff John nodded. He knew she was right. Whatever killed her didn't care about the fact she was old. And it had to have been another monster that did this. Even at her advanced age, Clara would have torn an ordinary human to pieces if they had threatened her.

About half an hour later, Bill Bennett pulled into the driveway with his large box truck. There was a ton of growling and snarling coming from inside and also a bunch of weight being thrown against the walls, causing the truck to rock back and forth.

As Bill stepped out of the truck, he pounded his fist on the side of the box and yelled at its cargo.

"Pipe down, you useless pieces of crap! I'll feed you to Buster if you don't stop!"

The sounds stopped almost immediately.

"Sheriff, how's it goin?" said Bill as he extended a very beefy, very hairy hand to Sheriff John.

Sheriff John shook his hand and said, "Well, Bill, being as how I called you out here with your hounds, you can guess it isn't going very well."

Bill looked at the house and asked, "So, what'd the old lady do this time?"

"I'm afraid that the *old lady* was murdered."

Bill's mouth dropped open and his eyes went dark with rage, as he looked at the house. The sheriff and the deputy could hear the low, guttural growl coming from his throat. Debbie saw fangs begin to be bared behind his lips. She reached out and placed a hand on his forearm.

"Bill, please."

Bill's head snapped toward her and there was a second of rage and growling, but it evaporated almost instantly. Debbie's hand stayed firmly on his arm.

Bill took a deep breath and calmed down.

"Sorry, Debbie."

"It's okay. It hurts me, too."

Sheriff John spoke up, "There's a trail of blood leading from the back of the house toward the trees. I need to see if you and your hounds can track it and see where it leads."

Bill nodded and then asked, "Do we know how long it's been since this happened?"

"No and that's going to be the biggest problem. From the looks of the scene inside, it's been at least a few days, but not much longer than a week. The blood is all dried, but it hasn't turned black like it would after ten days or so."

"That's a long time, sheriff."

"That's why I called you. If anyone is going to be able track that trail, it's you and your hounds."

Bill nodded and turned and headed to the back of his truck. They could hear him raise the back door of the box and Bill yelled at his hounds inside.

"You two better behave or I swear, Buster is going to eat good tonight!"

There was a little growling and a couple of barks, but neither the sheriff nor Debbie could tell it if was from the hounds or from Bill. After a couple of minutes there was a bit of a ruckus from the back of the truck and they turned to see Bill had jumped down, followed closely by two of the biggest, meanest looking hell hounds anyone had ever seen. They easily came to Bill's chest and he was a pretty big guy.

As they walked toward the two law officers, the hounds growled and snapped at each other. The chains attached to their collars were not the usual, prissy chains you might buy at PetSmart. These were heavy duty, link chains like you would hear if you heard Death shambling slowly down your hallway in the middle of the night.

"Knock it off!' yelled Bill.

Debbie stepped forward and reached out and ran her hands over one hounds head. Both of their heads were easily at the same level as Debbie's.

"Oh, Bosley, settle down. You're not as big and bad as you think you are."

Bosley looked at her and growled.

"Yeah, right." she said with a smile.

She reached over and scratched the ears of the other hound.

"Are you keeping him in line, Daisy?"

Daisy shook her massive head and growled.

"I know," said Debbie, "boys can be such a pain."

"We'll start at the back of the house," said the sheriff.

They walked around the house, with Debbie walking between the two hounds, holding onto their collars. They just walked easily along with her, like she was more their master than Bill. Of course, she was their friend.

When Bill led the two hounds to the back porch, they sniffed around the steps and the grass. Bosley sat down, raised his head and began a mournful howl. Daisy nuzzled up against his head and then she joined him in his grief.

After a few seconds, Bill said, "Let's find her."

The two hounds began pulling at their chains and heading toward the trees. Bill had his hands full trying to keep them under control, but he had done this a few times before. They knew who the boss really was.

The sheriff and deputy followed along behind them. Staying about ten feet back, they pulled their weapons and stayed alert. They didn't really expect to find anything dangerous out here after so much time had passed, but they didn't want to take any chances.

"You know, deputy, you don't need to come out here. Bill and I can handle this."

Debbie looked at her dad and said, "Look, I was just surprised at the amount of blood I found in the house and what it meant. I'm okay now."

"Well," said the sheriff, "I'm glad you are because I don't think I am."

She reached over and squeezed her dad's arm as they continued to follow the other three into the trees.

She still got a little riled up whenever her daddy would try to protect her in dangerous situations. She was more than capable of handling herself when it came to monsters. She just wished her daddy could admit that.

Bosley and Daisy had their noses to the ground and were growling and snarling as they moved along the path through the trees. It didn't take long to find what they were looking for.

In a small swale they found Clara's body, or what was left of it. Her clothes had been ripped to shreds and there wasn't much meat left on her bones. It was quite obvious that Clara had changed into a gargoyle during the attack and that was the skeleton they found.

However, they didn't find her head. It had been separated from the rest of her body and wasn't anywhere around.

Bill took the two hounds to a tree and wrapped their chains around a limb.

"Stay!" said Bill to the hounds.

They laid down and watched as the others approached the body. They didn't want to go anywhere near it. Hell hounds or not, a gargoyle had just been killed and they weren't too courageous at this point. If whatever had killed Clara was still in the area, they could very well be the next victims.

Sheriff John and Deputy Debbie moved across the swale to the remains of the body. Looking down at the bones, Debbie felt an overwhelming sense of wanting to shoot something. Clara had always been a good, kind woman to her and always had a smile whenever their paths crossed.

Bill walked over and looked down and said, "So, you think this is another monster that did this?"

The sheriff looked at him and then shook his head.

"Do you think it could be something else, Bill? She was a gargoyle, for crying out loud. A grizzly bear couldn't do this to her."

Debbie reached out and put a hand on her daddy's arm.

"Calm down."

"Sorry, sheriff. I guess I shouldn't be asking the obvious."

The sheriff looked at him and then felt bad for flying off the handle.

"No Bill, I'm sorry. I'm just not looking forward to what is about to become a very scary time here in Prattville."

"You think there may be more?" asked Debbie.

The sheriff crouched down and studied the bones a little closer.

"I hate to say it, but I don't think this will be the last killing we see. As far as we know, Clara had no enemies. So, whoever, or whatever did this, did it for no damn good reason other than to kill and eat. Whatever did this could have just as easily caught a deer up in the hills."

Debbie spoke up, "The head missing suggests a trophy. Unless we find her head somewhere around here, it's a good bet the killer took it."

"Oh man," said Bill, "You're not suggesting ..."

The sheriff jumped up and scowled at him.

"No one is suggesting anything right now."

Debbie reached out again and placed her hand on her daddy's arm.

"We don't know what happened here, but we can't ignore what happened twenty years ago."

The sheriff took a deep breath and closed his eyes. The last thing he needed was to face the fact that the horror of twenty years ago might be raising it's ugly head again.

He looked at Debbie and said, "Look, twenty years ago we had a terror go through this little town and scared the living bejeezus out of everyone and that's saying a lot about a town full of monsters."

Bill said, "You're preaching to the choir here, John. I'm a damn werewolf and the thought of what might be coming our way scares the hell out of me. But, we need to think about alerting the town and letting them know about this."

"Not just yet." said John. "Let's see if we can get a handle on what happened here before we start terrifying the townsfolk."

Then he reached up to his shoulder and keyed his mic, "Mabel, you out there?"

"Go ahead, sheriff."

"I need you to get on the horn to Chief Handley and tell him we need Chester out here to Clara's place."

"Will do, sheriff."

Chester was what passed for a crime scene

investigator in this area and he was quite well acquainted with monsters and what goes on around them. He had grown up near Prattville, the son of a demon and regular human woman, but he had no tendencies toward being a monster himself.

"Debbie, why don't you head back to the house and make sure it's taped off and keep anyone out that may come snooping around. When Chester gets here you can bring him back."

"Okay, sheriff." she said as she turned and started walking back toward the house.

After about a minute, Bill said, "Alright sheriff, you want to tell me why you did that? You know it will take Chester a good two hours to get here and no one ever comes out to Clara's place."

Sheriff John looked at the back of his retreating daughter and then turned to Bill.

"We're going hunting."

"Hunting?"

"That is correct. We're going to spend a little time seeing if we can track the killer."

Bill's eyes opened wide.

"Just the two of us?"

"No, just the four of us." said John as he motioned toward Bosley and Daisy.

Bosley saw that and raised his head, with his eyes wide open and then turned his head and buried it behind Daisy's shoulder. Daisy just looked at the sheriff and shook her head so fast slobber flew off her mouth in every direction.

"I don't know, sheriff. Deputy Debbie is correct when she says Bosley isn't all that tough and Daisy isn't much tougher. It's all sound effects and visual appearance that gets them the fear they crave. When it comes to taking them into battle, we'd be better off with Buster in his wiener dog state."

The sheriff looked at the two hell hounds and said, "You two are worthless."

Daisy dropped her head to the ground, looking up at the sheriff with pouting eyes.

"Don't say that sheriff." said Bill, "You'll give them a complex."

"Well, what good are hell hounds that don't strike the fear of Hell into a person?"

"Well, they're just fine with people. It's monsters that give them the heebie jeebies."

The sheriff crouched down and looked Daisy right in the eyes.

"You're pathetic."

She raised up and looked at the sheriff and her fangs began to show.

"But, I'm only asking you to track, not to fight."

He reached out and ran his hand up the side of her face and scratched behind her ear.

"Can you do that for me? Can you do it for Clara?"

Daisy looked over at the remains of the gargoyle and then back at the sheriff. She gave a short woof and jumped to her feet. Then she looked down at Bosley, who was still cowering on the ground. She leaned down and growled in his ear and he immediately raised his head and looked at her. His eyes were still filled with fear, but he reluctantly climbed to his feet.

As Bill was unwrapping their chains from the branch, the sheriff leaned in and whispered to the two hounds.

"And for what it's worth, I don't think you're worthless at all. I'd take either one of you over that mangy Buster any day."

Daisy leaned over and butted her head against the sheriff's shoulder. She knew he only called them out when there was something that needed their special expertise. She just wished it didn't include going after something capable of killing a gargoyle.

The two hounds walked over to where the bones were and sniffed around. In no time at all, the hounds picked up the trail that lead away from the kill site.

Turning and pulling at their chains, they led the way into the woods and before they had taken three breaths, the four of them disappeared into the trees.

Chapter 4
~~
Face to face with terror

Debbie looked down the hill, into the swale and there was a distinct lack of her father. Or Bill and his hounds, for that matter. The only thing still there were the bones of Clara.

"I thought you said Sheriff John was out here."

"He was here when I went back to the house to wait for you. I wonder where he's gotten off to?"

Chester had taken the better part of two hours to reach Prattville because he was involved in another case in Hobart. He loved coming to Monster Town, though. He had grown up about halfway between the two towns and had heard all the stories about the monsters that lived in the town just east of his family farm.

Of course, his parents had always denied there were monsters living in Prattville. According to them, there were no such things as monsters.

For a time Chester had believed them. Right up until the time he found out his father was a demon. Now, being a demon, you would think he would have a hard time with the ladies, but Chester's mom had seen right through his tough, demon exterior and saw a good spirit in there. It didn't take long for the two of them to fall in love, get married and Chester was the result.

Though he didn't have any monster tendencies of his own, Chester did know his way around the monster world and becoming a crime scene investigator seemed like a natural to him. Humans could be monsters all by themselves, without any of the monster traits.

They walked down into the depression and stopped next to Clara's bones and Chester started taking photos of the scene. While he was doing that, Debbie stepped off to the side and looked to the west.

"I hope daddy hasn't gone and done something foolish."

"Like what?" asked Chester as he continued snapping pictures.

"Like going off, looking for the killer by himself."

"He's not by himself."

"C'mon Chester. You know those two hell hounds aren't worth a damn in a fight."

"That may be true, but Bill is more than capable in a fight. He's got your daddy's back."

She turned back around and looked at Chester.

"I certainly hope so, but even with Bill, they're obviously looking for something that could take down a gargoyle. Bill might even have a bit of trouble with that."

"True," said Chester, as he crouched down to get a

better angle on some of the bones.

"Thanks, Chester. That gives me all kinds of confidence."

He looked at her and then stood up.

"I'm sorry Debbie, but your daddy is a more than capable law enforcement officer. He's seen his share of monsters and he's always handled them."

Debbie took a deep breath and nodded.

"That's okay. I'm just worried about him and Bill finding something even they can't handle."

She looked down at the corpse and asked, "Is there anything I can do to help?"

"You can just take notes on this as I call things out to you," he said as he handed her his clipboard.

Then he started moving around the scene, talking about what he was seeing. Debbie wrote down everything he said.

Chester pointed to some gouges in the ground.

"You see those gouges?"

"Yeah."

"I'm going to get a plaster cast of those, but I'd bet dollars to donuts that Clara made those during the fight."

"Are you sure?"

"Why? Do you have a better idea?"

"It just seems to me that she may have been killed before her body was even brought here. There's an awful lot of blood back in the house."

"That's true, but I'm thinking she didn't change into a gargoyle until after she was out of the house."

"What leads you to believe that?"

"Well, you saw the back door to her house."

"Yes?"

"If she had been a gargoyle when she was pulled through that doggy door, there would have been a lot more damage. I suspect that door would have been torn right off its hinges if she'd changed before going through it."

"Makes sense, I guess. What we really need to know is what kind of monster could kill a gargoyle, even one as old as Clara."

~~~~

Sheriff John, Bill and his hounds spent the better part of an hour sniffing along the trail Daisy and Bosley had picked up. After coming to a dead end, they decided it was best to turn back and get back to the crime scene.

"I don't understand how the trail could just go cold like that," said Bill. "These hounds may not be too tough when it comes to fighting monsters, but there are none better at following a trail."

The sheriff stood in the middle of a small clearing where the trail had run out. There were only three ways out of the clearing and one of those ways was the trail they had just come up on.

He knew another trail went down the hill and into the backside of the Taylor farm and the third trail went up into the hills. Though he knew a little about what was up there, he wasn't as familiar with it as he would have liked. He didn't fancy tramping around in that area without plenty of back up and a lot more daylight.

"I think we need to start heading back. It's gonna be dark soon and I don't want to be out here after the sun sets," said the sheriff. "Last thing I need is Debbie calling out the national guard to look for me."

Bill laughed and said, "Alright you two big babies, let's head back."

Bosley couldn't get turned around fast enough. He was ready to head back and crawl into the box truck and stay there until they got home. Daisy had to grab hold of his chain a couple of times to slow him down. Sometimes she wondered how she ever had a brother who was as big a chicken as Bosley.

As they started back, the sheriff took up the rear, letting the hounds and Bill set the pace going back. He was not ashamed to admit that right now, he was inclined to follow Bosley's lead and get out of these woods.

He couldn't quite put his finger on it, but he felt the hairs on the back of his neck standing up and that was never a good sign when you're surrounded by monsters. He couldn't shake the feeling that there was something watching them, but from some place hidden from his sight.

They made it to the edge of the clearing when all hell broke loose.

Passing under a tree, they heard a banshee scream and the sheriff looked up to see a dark figure dropping down out of the branches. It landed on him and knocked him down. He fought to stay conscious, but it was a losing battle. The last thing he saw was Daisy turning to the fight and growling meaner than even Buster was capable of doing.

Bill turned as he heard the scream and saw the dark figure land on top of the sheriff and he immediately went to his large Bowie knife that had been stuck down in his boot. He never got the chance to use it though.

The demon swept across the ground at him and was on him in the blink of an eye. He tried to bring the knife up to defend himself, but when he stabbed at the demon, the blade just went in like it was cutting through paper, but it had no effect on the dark figure.

The demon was about as tall as him, though not nearly as wide. But what it lacked in size it more than made up for in strength. It was quite clear this spawn of Hell was as strong as anything Bill had ever seen.

Daisy attacked and tried to rip the demon away from Bill, but she got flung across the path and up against a tree.

Bosley was the only one with a lick of sense and he tried to run. At first, Bill had a good hold on his chain, but when the demon attacked, he let go of the chain and it fell to the ground. Freed from his hold, Bosley took off as fast as he could down the path.

Daisy tried to get up, but she had suffered a broken back when she hit the tree and she couldn't move her back legs. She tried clawing her way forward as she saw Bill getting attacked, but she couldn't move very fast.

Bill tried to fight as hard as he could, but because it wasn't anywhere near the full moon, he couldn't make the change to werewolf, so he had to do battle as a man. A rather large man, but a man just the same.

Fighting as a man didn't stop him from fighting like a monster though. Slashing with everything he had, he got right into the face of the demon and tried to do his worst.

He looked at the demon, his face shrouded in the darkness of a hood over his head, but all he could see were two burning, red eyes staring back at him. Smelling the fetid breath of Death coming from inside the hood, he began to wonder if today was going to be his day to die.

As the demon grabbed him by the throat, Daisy was able to lunge forward and grab the demon by one of his ankles. The demon howled in pain as Daisy had finally found a place the demon would feel some pain. She bit down as hard as she could and the demon let go of Bill, dropping him in a heap on the ground.

The demon thrashed back and forth and then reached down and grabbed Daisy by the back of the neck and lifted her off the ground. Even though she was almost as big as a pony, the demon picked her up like she was a rag doll.

Bill could only watch as the demon ripped one of Daisy's legs off, bringing a screech of pain from the hell hound.

Bosley heard the screech and skidded to a stop on the path. He had already covered most of the distance back to the swale when he heard the scream of pain from his sister. He looked back over his shoulder, toward the sound of the battle.

Then he did something no one who knew him would have thought him capable of. He turned around and growled, looking back the way he had just come. Then his eyes lit up a bright, fiery red.

Like a shot from a cannon, he took off up that path and within seconds he rounded the final bend and saw the demon had a hold of his sister by the neck. As the fight came into view, he saw the demon rip another leg off Daisy and she thrashed about in pain, but it was a hopeless cause. He could hear the demon laughing as he reached for a third leg.

The demon never got the chance.

Bosley launched himself the last fifty feet between them and his mouth clamped down hard on the neck of the demon. Once a hell hound gets its teeth into you, it is never letting go and the only way to break their hold is to kill them. Bosley had no intention of making it that easy for the demon.

The demon lost its hold on Daisy and she fell in a heap right next to Bill. He was in such bad shape he couldn't hardly move himself, but he reached out and pulled Daisy toward him and wrapped his arms around her, curling his body up around hers.

He looked up through some very misty eyes and saw Bosley tearing at the demon and actually doing some damage.

One thing he noticed was the demon's long fingernails as it tried to do battle with the hell hound. The demon slashed at Bosley with his claw-like fingernails and he ripped great wounds in the hell hound's side, but Bosley wasn't giving up. He continued to hold onto the demon's neck.

The demon went to rake Bosley again and finally wrenched the hound away, but the hell hound was able to grab the black hand in his mouth and bite down hard. The sickening sound of bones being crushed could be heard throughout the woods.

The demon howled in pain and flung Bosley across the path, almost landing on top of the sheriff.

Bosley wasn't about to admit defeat. He charged the demon again, teeth bared, eyes blazing and growling as if it were coming from the very depths of Hell.

When he got close enough, the demon swiped at him, but missed completely. Bosley used that to his advantage and went for an ankle, grabbing hold, thrashing and swiveling in an effort to break his foot right off.

The demon decided he had had enough and he bashed Bosley on top of the head to break his hold. Then, the demon turned and fled into the woods. Bosley chased him for a few feet, but Bill called weakly to him.

When he heard the voice of his master calling, Bosley turned back and walked slowly across the path. He stopped and looked down at Bill and his sister. She was breathing, but it was very ragged. Bosley laid down on the ground and placed his nose right up to hers and whined.

Daisy opened her eyes slowly and stretched her nose out to his and they touched. Bosley whined again and Daisy gave him a little growl. This wasn't her usual *"get yer butt off the ground and get ready to fight"* growl. It was more of an *"it will be alright brother, be strong"* type of growl.

Bill still had his arms wrapped around her neck, trying to comfort her, but he knew she wasn't long for this world. Of course, she and Bosley weren't really from this world in the first place, but she was on her way home.

They all heard a bit of groaning behind them and Bosley raised his head and looked over to see Sheriff John was beginning to regain consciousness.

"Go check on the sheriff, buddy."

Bosley wasn't sure he wanted to leave his sister at that moment, but he did what he was asked and got up. He moved slowly across the path to where the sheriff was still trying to shake the cobwebs out of his head. He became quite alert when Bosley lowered his head and snuffled his wet, slobbery nose into the sheriff's face.

"Oh, damn! Alright Bosley, I'm awake," he said as he pushed the hound's face away.

The sheriff pushed himself up and began looking around and that's when he saw Bill and Daisy laying together a few yards away.

"Oh, no no no," he said as he scrambled to his feet and moved to them.

Looking down at the pair, the sheriff wasn't sure if he was going to be able to keep it together. Daisy was obviously near death, what with missing her two front legs and all. Bill looked like he had been put through a meat grinder, too.

He dropped to his knees and reached out and ran his hand over Daisy's head.

"Hey, big girl."

She opened her eyes a little and then turned her head slightly and licked his hand.

"I'm so sorry," he said.

He had to keep it together. He was the law in these here parts and crying just wouldn't do for a tough lawman.

It only took another few seconds and Daisy let out her last breath. Her body went limp and her head dropped to the dirt. Bill buried his face into the fur on the back of her neck and just held her tight. The sheriff could tell that even he, a big, bad werewolf, was having trouble maintaining his composure.

Bosley sat down on his haunches and raised his head and began a very long, low howl. It was loud and it was piercing and it drove all the birds from the trees. The sun was just setting in the west and the golden light was filtering through the trees and seemed to light up Daisy as she lay there.

"Sheriff, what's happening?"

Sheriff John had his head bowed and didn't hear. He was wondering what would have happened if he hadn't suggested tracking the killer.

"Sheriff! Are you okay?"

He snapped out of it when he felt Bill's hand on his arm.

"You better answer her," he said to the distraught sheriff.

He reached up and keyed the mic on his

shoulder.

"Yeah, Debbie. I'm here."

"What happened? I just heard one of the hounds baying."

"We've had a bit of an incident."

"Okay. Is everyone alright?"

"No, Debbie, we're not. We're ..."

Then the sheriff looked down and noticed that Bill was laying in a pool of blood and it only took a second to realize it wasn't Daisy's. The hell hound's blood was as black as used motor oil and Bill's was the normal red you would expect when he was in human form. It was that crimson color that was spreading out around the big man.

"Bill, you're hurt."

"Just a scratch, man. I'll be okay."

He moved around Daisy's head and began trying to get Bill to release her so he could get a look at his injuries. Bill just held on, not wanted to let go of one of his babies.

"Daddy?"

"Just a second, Debbie!" he yelled into his mic.

"Bill, let her go. I need to check you out."

Bill looked up at him and shook his head.

"There ain't nothing to be done, sheriff. Just promise me you'll find a good home for Bosley."

"What? No, his home is with you. Now let go of Daisy so I can tell Debbie what we need out here."

Bill didn't want to, but he slowly relaxed his hold on the hell hound and rolled onto his back. As he moved apart from Daisy, the sheriff got his first look at the gash that went all the way from Bill's waist to his armpit on his left side.

"Damn it, Bill! Just a scratch my ass!"

"I ain't scratchin' your ass," laughed Bill as he choked up some blood. "You scratch your own smelly ass."

"Debbie! We need the paramedics out here immediately!" he yelled into his mic. "Make sure to tell them it's Bill they are coming to help so they know what they need to bring."

"I'm on it, sheriff."

John looked down at Bill and could see some fear in his eyes. One thing Bill had never even considered was that he might die someday as an ordinary man.

"I guess he got me pretty good, John."

"Yeah, well, I've seen worse. You just try to relax and watch your breathing."

"Sheriff?"

"Yeah, Debbie, go ahead."

"The paramedics are on their way, but I need to know where to send them."

"We are about a mile west of you, right on the trail that comes up from behind Farmer Taylor's hog farm. You know which one I mean?"

"Yes, I do."

"We're right where that trail intersects with the east-west trail back to you."

"Alright, let me tell them. They should be able to get to within a couple hundred yards of you there."

"Alright. Tell them to make it quick. Bill's in a bad way."

As he turned back to Bill, the werewolf looked up at him.

"I thought you said you'd seen worse." he coughed out.

"I just told her that to get them paramedics moving faster."

"Listen, John."

"Nope, nope. You're not going to be telling me I need to watch after Bosley. That's your job."

"No sheriff. Listen to me."

Sheriff John stopped talking and leaned down to hear what he had to say.

"I saw his eyes. I also smelled his breath. If I was to guess, I'd say it was what the kids used to call the Boogerman."

"Red eyes? The smell of death on its breath?"

Bill nodded weakly. Then he closed his eyes and let his body relax. John reached out and shook his shoulder.

"Hey, no sleeping!"

"Relax, sheriff. I'm just trying to conserve my energy. I don't want to die, but I may not have a choice in the matter."

Then Bill kind of laughed, very weakly, but it was a laugh.

"What could you possibly find funny right now?" asked the sheriff.

"Oh, just the thought of you trying to figure out what to do with Bosley after I'm gone."

"That is not funny!"

Bill cracked one yellow eye and looked at him.

"It's a little funny."

"Sheriff, I'm on my way to you!"

The sheriff snatched at his mic and yelled, "Oh no you're not! You get back to the house and get yourself weaponed up. Also, get on the horn and get Cal out here and tell him to come loaded for bear. You might consider calling anyone else you think might be able to help us with this."

"Alright, I'll get some weapons and get Cal on the way to where you are. But, tell me, what are we dealing with?"

The sheriff didn't know if wanted to tell her, but he knew he had to. If for no other reason than to make her aware of how serious it was.

"Debbie, it looks like it's the Boogerman."

There were a few seconds of silence and then she came back, with a much smaller voice.

"Understood, sheriff. I'm going to clear Chester out of here and then I'm driving my truck around to where you are."

"That'll work."

As he let go of the mic, he could hear the far off siren of the paramedics coming down the highway, looking for the turnoff.

"Just hold on, Bill. They're almost here." he said as he patted him on the shoulder.

Bill reached up weakly and patted his hand.

"Don't blame yourself for this, John. It wasn't your fault."

In his radio he could hear Mabel come on.

"Deputy, you don't worry about anything, but getting around there to the sheriff. I'll call Cal and I think the Johnson boys will be best to call out for this."

"Thanks, Mabel."

The sheriff sat down next to the fallen werewolf and rested a hand on his shoulder. Bosley laid down next to him and sniffed at Bill's head. The last thing this big, bad hell hound wanted was to lose his entire family in one night.

Chapter 5
~~
Meeting a new ally

The sheriff looked up from his desk. His daughter was standing on the other side of the desk, with her hands on her hips.

"Daddy, I don't think keeping Bosley here in the station is going to work."

"Well, just exactly what do you expect me to do with him? I can't just turn him out onto the streets. I can't put a bullet in his head."

"Of course not! He saved your life!"

"I know that! Don't you think I know that?"

Debbie looked at him, fuming a little bit that he had even considered a thought like that. Ever since Bosley had lost his sister, he had been laying around, not doing much of anything. Debbie felt sorry for him and wanted to do something to help.

"Just what is it you think we should do with him?" asked the sheriff.

"Let me take him home. He can stay with me until we find a better solution to the problem."

"Take him home?" bellowed the sheriff. "Let me get this straight. You want to take a hell hound home, like he's some stray puppy?"

"Why not? What do you think is going to

happen?"

"Oh gee, let me see. He could destroy your house, he could scare the bejeezuz out of anyone that comes to your door and, oh yeah, he could kill you!"

"Bosley?!" she yelled. "Bosley wouldn't kill me anymore than you would."

She leaned over and looked the sheriff right in the eyes.

"You wouldn't kill me, would you, daddy?"

The sheriff sat back in his chair and started rubbing his chin.

"Daddy?"

"I'm thinking!" said the sheriff.

"Sheriff John!" yelled Mabel. She had been sitting at her desk, trying to stay out of it and trying to keep from laughing.

"What, Mabel?!"

"Don't you take that tone with me, young man."

"Sorry. I lost my head."

"I think the deputy makes a good point. Bosley can't stay downstairs. We need those cells for those that deserve to be in them. Bosley does not."

"No kidding." said Debbie. "Yesterday you stuck a couple of kids in the cell next to him and when I checked on them this morning, they had, well, let's just say it's going to be awhile before that smell goes away."

"He just scared them a little."

"A little? He scared the shit out of them! Literally!"

"Okay, so they won't be coming back to Prattville anytime soon, looking for monsters."

Deputy Debbie threw her hands in the air and screamed, "Agghhhh."

The sheriff just laughed as she turned around and searched for something to hit. When she heard him laughing, she spun around and glared at him.

"What are you laughing about?"

"I just think it's kinda cute when you get all flustered like this."

Debbie's mouth dropped open and she was ready to release the mother of all tirades on her father, but he beat her to the punch.

"Of course, you can take Bosley home. If for no other reason than to let him watch over you."

She lowered her hands and stood there.

"Do you mean it?"

"Sure I mean it. With that monster still out there, I'd rather you had someone at your place to keep an eye on things. Bosley's already proven he can go toe-to-toe with this Boogerman monster."

Just then Cal came walking into the station, followed by Jake, one of the Johnson boys.

"Any luck today, Cal?" asked the sheriff.

"Nope, not a damn thing. If he's still in the area, he's gone to ground and we won't find him until he resurfaces."

"Alright, I think we can call off the searches of the mountainside. Jake, Bill being a friend of yours, we're thankful for your help."

"Glad I could help, sheriff. You can go ahead and call off the search, but my brother and me are probably gonna keep looking for another day or so."

"Well, you and Randy be careful up there. I know you two can handle yourselves, but that Boogerman went through me and Bill and Daisy like we were little kids."

"Will do, sheriff." said Jake as he turned and headed out the door.

Cal turned and left, heading back out to his regular patrol. After he was gone, Debbie sat down across from her father.

Her dad looked at her and said, "We need to be careful about this getting out. I know we need to alert the townsfolk, but I worry about it getting back to your friend, Cindy."

"I do, too. This might scare her right back into her nightmares."

"Have you talked to her since the attack at Clara's house?"

"No, not yet. I was supposed to go over to Hobart and see her and her son that evening, but this attack has put that on the back burner."

"Well, you need to talk to her so she doesn't hear

about this through the grapevine. She, above anyone else, needs to hear about this and it's probably best if it comes from you."

Debbie nodded and stood up.

"I agree and I think it needs to be done in person. It's close to the end of my shift, so I think I'll take a drive to Hobart and visit her."

Sheriff John nodded, "You just be careful."

"Okay, sheriff." she said as she turned and headed out the door.

~~~~

The drive to Hobart took about an hour and a half and the entire way there, she was playing the conversation through in her head that she hoped she would have. The problem with that kind of thinking is, the other party most likely will not be reading from the same script, so your carefully planned conversation is likely to be derailed no sooner than it gets started.

Pulling into Hobart just after the sun had gone down, she worked her way across town. Chief Handley and Cindy lived on the western edge of Hobart. Debbie was berating herself the whole time, because she really did like visiting their home. Cindy had made a very nice home, complete with a beautiful flower garden, some small farm animals and quite a few fruit trees. It was just the kind of place meant for raising a small family.

Her son, Toby, was just three years old and Debbie couldn't believe she hadn't seen him in over a year and she was quite sure he was going to be almost grown up by the time she saw him again.

After talking with Cindy on the phone the week before, she knew she never again wanted to go more than a week or two without seeing her friend. Tonight, she was going to get to see her for the first time in over a year.

She reached the property and turned into the drive and went back toward the house. The house sat about a hundred yards off the highway and Cindy had planted dozens of rose bushes along each side of the driveway, so when they were in full bloom, you were driving through a rainbow of color to get to the house.

As she pulled up to the house, she was dismayed to see that it was quite dark. It was obvious there was no one home.

She got out of her truck and made the walk up the steps to the front door and knocked. She waited about thirty seconds, but she knew there was going to be no answer. She really felt like kicking herself for not calling first, but she didn't want to have to explain why she was making the trip.

As she was getting ready to turn and head down

the steps and back to her truck, she saw some headlights coming up the drive and as they got closer, she saw it was a police car. At first she thought it might be Chief Handley coming home, but as they parked and the headlights went out, she could see it was one of the other police officers.

She walked down the steps toward her truck as the officer climbed out of his car.

"Deputy, how are you doing this evening?" said the officer.

"Officer, Jeffers, wasn't it?"

"Yes, ma'am. Kind of surprised you would remember that, having only met for a few seconds a couple of weeks ago."

"Well, I know I may have made an impression on you and the other officer, so I do remember your name. Anyway, I made the trip out here to visit with Cindy, but it appears I may have made the trip for nothing."

"I hate to say it, but Chief Handley and his family are gone on vacation. Left a couple of days ago and won't be back for about three weeks."

"That's actually good news." said Debbie with a sigh of relief.

"Good news?"

"Well, I have something I need to discuss with Cindy and it may cause her some undue stress. If she won't be back for three weeks, that situation will be handled and she won't even need to know about it."

"You talking about that time she was abducted as a kid?"

"You know about that?"

"Yes, ma'am. It's not really a secret around here."

"Okay, I am going to need you to be very careful what you say to her if you see her or talk to Chief Handley before I do. This could very well bring up memories for her that she may not be ready to handle if it's just dropped on her."

"How about, if I talk to Chief Handley, I just ask him to have his wife call you, that you just wanted to visit with her?"

"That would work."

She looked around the property in the growing dark and took a deep breath.

"It's so peaceful out here."

"Yes it is. She likes it that way."

"I just want to make sure it stays that way for her."

Jeffers nodded and then asked, "Can I ask you a question?"

"Shoot."

"What kind of deputy sheriff are you?"

"I don't understand your question, Officer Jeffers. I'm just a deputy to my father who is the sheriff of Prattville."

"No, I understand that. It's just that incident that

happened a couple of weeks ago ... I know what I saw coming down that highway, but I had no way of proving it. And those weapons I saw in the back of this truck? Well, they don't look like any weapons I'm familiar with."

Debbie had a bit of a smile on her face, trying to figure out what she could and couldn't say to this man. She decided to show him. So she walked around the back of her truck and opened the tailgate. He watched as she punched in her code on an electronic keypad and then stepped back as the floor in the back of the truck levered up and a light came on over the concealed compartment.

Jeffers let out a soft whistle as he saw all the different weapons, loaded into various holders and racks. Just as before, most of them were glowing or had bright, red power indicators. He doubted there was anything in there that even knew what gunpowder smelled like.

He looked at Debbie and said, "This is why I ask, what kind of deputy are you? That monster dog we saw a couple of weeks ago? I'm guessing a regular gun with regular bullets wouldn't have done much of anything to slow him down."

"Officer Jeffers, you're absolutely correct. And I need to tell you right now, if my daddy knew I was showing you this or telling you anything, he'd probably take me out behind the barn and tan my hide."

He reached up and did the zipper across the lips movement and Debbie laughed a little.

"There are such things in this world as monsters. Just like Buster. He's just a harmless, little, wiener dog most of the time, but when it gets close to the full moon, well, let's just say he can become a real handful."

"Oh man, monsters?"

"Yes, sir. And Buster isn't the only one living in Prattville."

"Really? There's more than just him?"

"Absolutely. A whole mess of 'em over in Prattville."

"So, that's why they call it Monster Town. I thought it was something else."

"Really? What did you think it was?"

'I was thinking it was because of your father."

"My father? Why in the world would he be the reason Prattville is nicknamed Monster Town?"

"Well, I've heard rumors he's pretty scary sometimes."

Debbie just laughed as she reached in and closed the weapon's vault. As she closed the tailgate on her truck, she looked back at Jeffers and shook her head.

"My daddy is just a big, teddy bear."

"I meant no offense."

"Oh, I know. I just think it's funny there's a rumor

going around that Monster Town is so named because of him. That's priceless."

She continued laughing as she walked around to the driver's side door.

"Maybe I could buy you dinner in the next day or so and you could tell me all about what you do and what your days are like."

She stopped and looked at him.

"Why, Officer Jeffers! Are you asking me out on a date?"

"Uh, well ..." he stammered, but couldn't get any more words to squeeze out of his mouth.

She laughed again as she climbed into her truck.

"Okay, but you're going to have to pass the test."

"What test is that?" he asked, fearing he might have made a grave mistake.

"You're going to have to come to MONSTER TOWN to take me out." she said with a bit of a haunting laugh, to emphasize those two words. Then she laughed even more.

He drew a breath and began to wonder if he was really up to this or not. Asking her out was something he had considered ever since that day two weeks ago, when he first saw her. But, now that he knew about Monster Town, he wasn't sure if he had it in him to go through with it.

"I can do that," he said with a slight shake in his voice.

She giggled a little more as she turned the key and started up the hot rod engine she had under her hood.

"How about tomorrow night?" he asked.

"Tomorrow night? No. Not good, but the next night would be perfect."

"Okay, Thursday night it is, say six o'clock? Where should I meet you in 'Monster Town'?" he said, drawing some air quotes to emphasize the name of the town.

"Just meet me at the sheriff's office."

"Great. I'll see you there."

"Good night, Officer Jeffers."

"Good night, deputy."

She put the truck into Reverse and made a quick three point turn around the back of his cruiser and drove back out the driveway and hit the road back to Monster Town. All the way home, she had a smile on her face. This was going to be her very first date, since returning to Prattville almost four years ago.

And he was kind of cute, too.

~~~~

Later that night, as she was sleeping quietly in her own bed, she had a dream she would rather not have had. One thing that always surprised her, even though she lived in a town full of monsters, was she never had nightmares. Not once.

Until tonight.

She found herself back in the third grade, back to being a nine-year-old girl and back to having her best friend taken by the Boogerman. She tried everything she could to get the adults to listen to her, but she couldn't get them to understand. They all told her that Cindy had just run away. They all told her that there was no such thing as monsters.

Then she found her friend herself, but in this nightmare, she found Cindy's dismembered body in the barn. She had been torn to pieces and the whole barn was covered in her blood. As Debbie walked into the barn, seeing her friend like this, she felt the hairs on the back of her neck stand up and when she turned around, the Boogerman was right there and grabbed her by the throat.

She tried to fight him off, but he just laughed in her face and then used his long fingernails to rip her body to pieces. The last thing he did was cut her head off and hold it up in front of him and looked into her eyes.

"You can't save her. I will have her this time," growled the demon.

She blinked her eyes and then screamed.

Then next thing she knew, she was sitting up in her bed, covered in sweat and breathing hard. She looked around and it took a few seconds to realize she was in her own bedroom.

As she looked around again, she was startled to see two burning, red eyes looking at her. She jumped and landed on her feet on the opposite side of the bed. As her feet hit the floor, she grabbed her gun she kept in a holster wedged between the mattresses and pointed it at the eyes that seemed to be following her.

"Who are you?" she yelled.

She saw the eyes blink, but there was no reply.

She yelled again.

"Who are you and how did you get in here?"

Still no answer. Just two red eyes, seemingly floating in the darkness.

"Listen, you better start talking before I blow you right straight to Hell."

Woof.

"What?!"

Woof.

"Oh good grief." she yelled as she reached and turned on the bedside lamp.

"Bosley! How did you get in here?"

The big, black hell hound just stared at her, or more precisely, stared at the gun she had pointed right between his eyes.

Woof.

"Oh, sorry." said Debbie as she lowered the gun and put it back in the holster.

Walking around the bed, she reached out and

scratched Bosley behind the ear.

"You know, this would go a lot smoother if you'd learn to talk."

Bosley looked at her and whined. Then he turned and walked out of the bedroom and through the living room, stopping at the front door.

"You need to go out?" she said as she walked up behind him.

Woof.

She opened the door and let him out. After he clambered down the steps and into her front yard, she walked out onto the porch and sat down in her favorite chair. She watched as Bosley moved from plant to plant, probably looking for the best candidate to get sprinkled.

"Gawd, I hope he doesn't kill my trees and roses with that hell hound pee."

A few minutes later, after he had finished his business, he climbed back up the steps and laid down next to her. He kept his head up and alert, always checking the view in front of him.

She reached out and scratched his ear again and he leaned toward her, so she could get both sides.

"You like that, don't you?"

She looked out across the yard, toward the road. It was just after two in the morning, so there was no traffic at all.

She heard Bosley whimper just a little.

"What's the matter, Boz?"

He looked over her and had a sad look in his eyes, which Debbie found amazing, considering he had the burning, eyes of a hell hound.

"You miss Bill and Daisy, don't you?"

He whimpered again and laid his head down on the floor next to her chair, which put the top of his head about even with her shoulders.

"Yeah, I miss them too, buddy. But, you can stay here as long as you need to."

Bosley grunted and then she heard him snoring.

"Until Hell calls and sends you to a new home, I guess," she said softly, still rubbing his head.

She looked out across the yard and let her thoughts drift back to the dream.

She knew it was a dream, but it had seemed so real. One other thing about this dream was, it didn't fade like dreams usually do. She could still remember it like it was a movie she had just watched. She could remember every detail.

The Boogerman seemed to be there especially for her, taunting her. Letting her know that no matter what she did, she couldn't stop what was coming.

What she really didn't like was how Cindy had figured so prominently in the dream. Dismembered and dead.

Then something occurred to her. The Cindy in this dream was not the nine year old Cindy from her childhood. It was the grown up Cindy she knew now.

Why would she be seeing the grown up Cindy killed by the Boogerman in her dreams?

The thought terrified her. Maybe it wasn't just a dream, but a premonition of things to come. Was Cindy still in danger?

Well, it didn't matter. Cindy and her family were gone for the next three weeks and she was going to do whatever she could to bring this to a close before her friend returned from vacation.

~~~~

Debbie jerked awake and found herself still sitting in the chair on the front porch. She was a bit chilled sitting out there in a pair of short shorts and a cropped t-shirt.

She looked around and noticed she was alone on the porch.

"Bosley?"

No answer.

"Bosley!"

Then came the pounding of paws and she stood up, trying to figure out where it was coming from. She began to realize she was standing there, half naked and without any weapon at all.

In a couple of seconds, Bosley came loping around the corner of the house and he had a small deer in his mouth.

"There you are. I was worried."

She turned to head into the house to get ready for the day and Bosley came walking up the steps.

"Oh, no you don't. You are not bringing your breakfast into the house! You can eat it out here. Just don't go anywhere. You'll scare the neighbors."

Bosley retreated to the lawn under one of the trees and began to munch on the deer. Debbie shook her head and went into the house.

"I wonder if Buster eats animals like that?" she wondered to herself.

Chapter 6

~~

Date night with a side of beating

As Debbie and Jeffers took their seat at the small restaurant in town, she couldn't help noticing how he kept looking around.

"Maybe it was a mistake to have dinner with you here in Prattville."

Officer Jeffers turned back to her and asked, "What? Oh, why do you say that?"

"Well, because ever since I told you about this little town you've been wondering how much of it is true and now, you're going to spend the entire evening wondering who is and who isn't a monster."

"I'm sorry." said Jeffers. "You're right. I need to pay more attention to you."

Debbie smiled as he asked her to trade seats in the booth. Now his back would be to the open room of the restaurant and she would be the main focus of his attention.

As they resettled themselves, she asked, "So, have you heard anything from the Handleys since the other night?"

"No, not really. Of course, I wouldn't expect to. They went on vacation, so I don't expect the chief would be checking in with me."

"No, I'm sure he wouldn't."

"Is it really that important for you to talk to Mrs. Handley?"

"I would like to, so I can tell her some things she should hear from me and not through the grapevine."

"I'll talk to Edna tomorrow. She's the woman that runs the department. If the Chief does call in, he'll talk to her. I'll let her know to have Mrs. Handley call you if the chief does call."

"Thanks. I'd appreciate that."

Just then the waitress came up to get their order and after she walked away, Debbie just smiled and looked at Jeffers.

"What are you smiling about?"

"Oh, it's just that you're so interested in looking out for monsters and one just took your order."

Jeffers turned and looked toward the waitress as she disappeared through the door and into the kitchen.

"Her?" he said pointing at the door. "She looked like a normal human being to me."

'They all do, Officer Jeffers."

"Please, call me Tom."

"Okay, Tom. The monsters that live here in Prattville are just normal, every day people most of the time and they just want to live their lives quietly and without any trouble."

"And that's where you and the sheriff's

department come in?"

"Exactly. We just try to keep things quiet around here."

"Until a big monster, demon dog gets loose and comes barreling toward the next town over," he said with a grin.

"Yep. Oh, that Buster, I'll tell you. One of these days daddy's gonna blast him into complete nothingness."

"Having seen the weapons in your truck, I imagine you both have weapons that could do just that."

"We have our toys."

They talked some more and then their meals came and Tom found himself watching the waitress as she walked away.

"Eyes front, sailor."

"Oh. Right. Sorry."

After they spent the next hour getting to know each other, they got up to leave and as they were walking out the front door, Tom bumped into a large guy. A really, large guy. And Tom was no shrimp, standing at six feet one inch tall.

"Sorry, pardon me," said Tom as he looked up at the man.

"You better watch where you're going, buddy." said the large man, leaning down and getting into Tom's face.

Tom leaned back, wondering what kind of monster he was dealing with here.

"Billy Ray?"

The large man straightened up and saw Debbie step out from behind Tom. He backed up about three steps and his eyes went wide open.

"Sorry deputy! I didn't mean noth ..."

"How are you doing tonight?" she said as she stepped up in front of the giant of a man.

Tom could see the man start to tremble and his voice got very shaky as he looked down at the short deputy.

"I"m ... I'm doing okay ... deputy. Just … looking to get something to eat."

"Well," she said as she reached out and patted him on the arm, "don't let us keep you. You have a good evening."

Billy Ray stepped around her, keeping a wary eye on her, as he made his way through the door Tom was holding open for him.

After the door closed and Tom was walking Debbie to her truck, he asked, "I have to ask, what was that all about?"

"Oh, Billy Ray. We've have had a couple of run ins. He's a good guy. He just needs to be watched every now and then."

As they reached her truck he held out his hand and when she took it to shake, he raised it to his lips and kissed the back.

"Why, Officer Jeffers. A kiss on the very first date," she said with a smile.

"I have to say, I like you, Debbie. I hope we can see each other again."

"I'd like that."

~~~~

When Debbie pulled into her drive, she could see Bosley laying on the front porch, right where she left him. She hadn't bothered to chain him to the post on the porch and sure as hell wasn't going to keep him locked up in the house. She just gave him a command to stay on the property while she was gone and hoped he would follow orders.

She saw his head raise and his red eyes start burning brighter as her headlights swept across the porch. Standing up, he shook himself to wake his body up. She noticed that when he shook his massive body, dust fell off the porch, meaning he was shaking the entire house.

"Oh Boz, I hope my little house can survive you."

Now she began to understand why Bill had bought a large, metal building and turned that into his home. It would have taken a lot for those two hell hounds to wreck that place.

Worried that one good sneeze from Bosley could

bring her whole house down, she knew Bosley would be standing in the middle of the wreckage, looking around like, "What did I do?"

As she turned off her truck's engine and got out, Bosley came sauntering down off the porch to greet her.

"Did you have a good day, Boz?"

Looking her right in the eyes, she could still see the sadness.

"I know, it's tough, buddy. But, it will get better with time."

She reached up and scratched his ear and then started walking up the steps to the house. As he went to follow her, she turned and looked at him.

"Have you finished your business out here?"

Woof.

"Did you get something to eat?"

Woof.

He turned his head and looked to a spot just off the end of the porch and she looked and saw another carcass of a dead deer.

"You know, we're going to have to figure something out or there won't be any deer left in the woods back there."

She opened the door and stepped inside and waited for the hell hound to squeeze his big body through the doorway. It was such a tight fit, he left some hairs stuck in the wood.

"Oh, man," she said as she plucked the hairs out of the door frame.

She held up the tufts of hair in front of his face and said, "You're gonna need to lose some weight, Boz."

She closed the door and headed for the kitchen to make a pot of tea. It wasn't quite time to go to bed and she was a little keyed up anyway. Her date with Tom had gone well and she could tell he liked her and she liked him.

"Just take it slow and easy." she mumbled to herself as she filled her tea kettle.

She looked out the window over the sink and all she could see was darkness. It was the night of the new moon, so there wouldn't be any moonlight shining on the fields behind her house.

As she lit the stove and set the kettle over the fire, she heard a scream. It was a scream unlike any she had ever heard before. It sounded like a wild animal was attacking another wild animal and one of them was losing the battle.

She ran to the back door and Bosley was right behind her. She opened the door and let the hell hound out. Bosley rushed past her and disappeared into the darkness.

She reached over and flipped open a wood panel on the wall and placed her hand over a black sheet of glass. The glass lit up and it read her hand print and when it had verified who she was, there was a click and another panel on the wall slid open.

She reached in and pulled out a glowing pistol that had a barrel about a foot long and about as big around as a baseball bat. She also pulled out a small radio headset and slipped it over her ear.

Running down the steps, she knew she was venturing into a very dangerous situation, being the only law in the area.

As she ran, she reached up and pressed a button on the earpiece.

"Cal, yeah, hey buddy, I need you."

After a few seconds she said, "Yeah, something's going on in the fields behind Farmer Smith's place."

Another scream ripped the silence of the night and this one was followed by a loud roar. Both were so loud that Cal could even hear them over the radio.

Debbie came to the fence between her property and Famer Smith's land and she was happy that the old farmer believed in the old ways. There was a stile directly in her path and she climbed up and over it, without having to deal with the barbed wire.

Of course, if she had been like Bosley, she would have just cleared it in one leap. That crazy hell hound launched himself from about twenty yards away and sailed easily over the fence and pounded away into the darkness.

After she jumped down from the stile and took

off running after the hound, she flipped a switch on the pistol she was carrying and a light came on, shining forward like a flashlight.

She flipped another switch and a low hum started coming from the weapon, which started to rise in pitch and as it did, the glow from the barrel of the pistol started to pulsate and changed from a light blue to a pink and she knew it would finish as a bright, blood red.

As she ran through the field, following the trail through the grain that Bosley had carved, she could hear what sounded like an intense battle between two combatants. Screams and roars shattered the night calm.

The scream was one she knew all too well. It was the sound of the Boogerman, though no one knew what kind of monster it was. It had been seen and heard, but not well enough to make an ID.

The roar was from a windigo, which could only mean one thing: Farmer Smith was involved in this battle.

A windigo is a beast that used to be a human, but changed when they ate human flesh. Their bodies wasted away, leaving nothing but rotted skin and muscle hanging off their skeleton.

Farmer Smith didn't become a windigo as a result of eating human flesh. He had been born that way, the child of two windigo beasts. He was able to stay in human form and that's just how he liked it, but if he were cornered or attacked, he could change in a heartbeat. And it sounded like that heartbeat had occurred many beats ago.

The next sound Debbie heard as she raced toward the battle, was the sound of Bosley joining the fray. The hell hound had reached the fight and she could hear him growl as he jumped into the middle of the mayhem.

Debbie finally reached the scene of the battle and it was as horrific as she thought it would be. Bosley was latched onto the Boogerman and taking a lot of shots from the demon.

She looked around and saw Farmer Smith laying on the ground, all cut to pieces and bloody. She could see he was still breathing and trying to move, but he was pretty torn up.

A screech from the Boogerman brought her back to reality and she leveled her weapon at the dark figure and squeezed the trigger. The ball of light slammed into the demon's shoulder and knocked him down and Bosley pounced on him with all the fury of Hell. He remembered this dark demon as being the one that took his family away from him and he wanted to have his pound of flesh. Or demon meat. Or whatever this foul creature was made of.

The creature slammed his fingers into Bosley's side, burying his fingernails all the way to his fingertips. Bosley screamed in pain, as the demon twisted the nails and pulled them out to drive them in again.

Debbie was running across the opening and got there just as the Boogerman climbed to his feet and shot at him again. He moved out of the way and then charged her before she could get another shot off. He barreled right into her, knocking her down and dropping on her.

She looked up and could see his red eyes and could smell his breath and he leaned down to put his face as close to her as he could. She couldn't see anything in the darkness under his hood, other than the red eyes staring back at her.

"I shall rip everything you love away from you," growled the demon, "and then I will rip your beating heart out of your chest!"

She broke one hand free and drove her fingers toward the red eyes as she yelled, "Bring it, jackass!"

He turned his head away at the last second and she felt his face. She could tell his skin was rotten and decaying, as her fingers drove right through his cheek and past his teeth. He screeched and rose up and was ready to go ahead and end her, even without making her suffer the loss of her loved ones.

He was ready, until Bosley clamped his jaws down on his ankle and bit down as hard as he could. Then, the hell hound started pushing himself backward on the ground, dragging the demon off Debbie. The Boogerman screeched in pain and tried to reach down and get his hands on the head of the hound, but he was being dragged so fast that he was just along for the ride.

Debbie climbed to her feet and looked around for her gun and saw it about twenty yards away. If it hadn't been for the glow, she may never have found it. She ran to it and bent over to pick it up, but she felt the world start to spin.

Fighting through the dizziness, she grabbed the pistol and ran toward where Bosley had dragged the Boogerman. As she was running, she heard a loud thump and a groan of pain and she could tell it was the hell hound.

As she got to the big dog, she found him laying on the ground, unconscious, but breathing. Spinning all around, she tried to find the Boogerman, but he was gone. She knelt down next to Bosley and ran her hand over his head.

"C'mon buddy. Don't be dying on me."

She heard him snort and saw one of his red eyes open. It was quite a bit dimmer than she would have liked and she wasn't too happy about the way he was breathing either.

"Deputy!"

"Over here, Cal!" she yelled as she stood up and shined her light toward the sound of his voice.

Cal came running up, with a large glowing rifle hanging over his shoulder. He stood about as tall her daddy and he was just as wide.

As he reached her, he saw she was about to fall down and reached out and grabbed her by the arm.

"Easy there, soldier." he said as he helped her sit down on a rock. "Where is he?"

"I don't know. He beat Bosley and by the time I got there, he was gone."

Cal walked over and knelt down next to the hell hound and ran his hand over his head. Then he stood up and pulled out his cell phone and hit speed dial.

"Hey, Kyle. Yeah, it's me. Hey, Bosley's been injured by the Boogerman and we need you to come and get him. Yeah, we're in the fields about two hundred yards behind Farmer Smith's house. Alright, we'll be watching for you."

He hung up and then dialed another number.

"Hey John, you need to ..."

Debbie began waving her hands wildly, trying to get him to stop talking to her dad. The last thing she wanted was for her daddy to think she couldn't handle herself. Or even worse, think she needed to move into his house until this all blew over.

"Debbie, I can't keep this from him," said Cal as he turned back to the phone.

"Yeah, John get to the fields behind Farmer Smith's place. Debbie had a little run in with the

Boogerman. Yeah, she's fine, just a little banged up. Alright, see you then."

Then he dialed another number.

"Yeah, this is Deputy Worhl. I need the paramedics to the fields behind Farmer Smith's place. He's been injured quite badly. Yeah, bring whatever you need. You actually have two to transport."

Debbie was fighting the urge to pass out as he finished all his calls. She looked up at him and even though her eyes were starting to cloud over, she saw a giant of a man.

"You're a real take charge kind of guy, Cal."

"Well, I learned it from you."

She let out a little laugh as she slipped down off the rock and landed on the ground. Cal knelt down in front of her and reached up and lifted her head by the chin.

"Hey, no going to sleep on me, sergeant."

"Sorry, corporal. I'm just feeling really tired."

"Yeah well, trying to take on a demon from Hell by yourself will kind of take it out of you."

They could hear a siren coming down the highway and then a few seconds later, another one. It took a couple of minutes for the paramedics and the sheriff to make their way across the fields, following the light Cal was waving at them.

Both units rolled to a stop together and all vehicle occupants bailed out.

"Where's Debbie?" yelled the sheriff.

"I'm right here, daddy." she said weakly.

He ran to her as the paramedics began working on Farmer Smith. The fact that they were dealing with windigo didn't slow them down a bit. Dealing with sick and injured monsters was not something new for them.

Sheriff John knelt down in front of Debbie and reached out and ran his hand over her cheek.

"Hey kiddo. How ya feeling?"

"Like I've been beaten half to death with a tree," she said as she fought to keep her eyes open. She wasn't going to let her daddy see her in any kind of weakness.

"I know exactly how you feel, baby. When he jumped on me a few days ago I felt like I had been hit by a truck."

"Mack or Peterbilt?" she asked and then laughed softly.

"Yeah, you're gonna be okay," he said as he patted her on the shoulder.

Then one of the paramedics came over and started tending to her and the sheriff stood up and looked around the battlefield. He saw another set of lights coming across the field and was surprised to see Kyle Manning come driving up in his big truck. He was even more surprised when Kyle got out of the truck, walked around the front fender and was followed by a little wiener dog.

"You brought Buster?" he gasped as he looked at Kyle.

"Take it easy sheriff. The full moon is a long ways off."

"It's not the full moon I'm worried about."

Buster made a beeline between the sheriff's legs and stopped to sniff at Debbie a couple of times. She reached out weakly and scratched his head.

"Hey buddy, go say hi to Bosley over there."

Buster yipped and then ran over to the injured hell hound. Bosley's eyes were closed and his breathing was really ragged, as Buster started sniffing around his face.

Then Buster growled at the big, devil dog and Bosley's eyes flew wide open. When he saw Buster looking at him, he raised his head and pulled back and away from the little hot dog.

"Hey, Bosley," said Kyle as he walked up. "I thought I'd bring a friend to check on you."

"That is so uncool, Kyle," groaned Debbie as the paramedics were getting ready to lay her on the gurney. "You know Bosley is terrified of Buster."

"I know that," said Kyle with a grin. "I figured if anyone could get a rise out of this hell hound, it would be Buster."

Then he turned back to Bosley and said, "Hey buddy, what's say we get you into the back of my truck and get you home. I'm sure the missus will have something to help get you right again."

Bosley looked at him and then back at the wiener dog that was just looking at him. He wasn't quite sure he wanted to go anywhere with this little dog. His eyes were as big as dinner plates.

"C'mon buddy, get up before I tell Buster to get you up."

The hell hound began to struggle and was finally able to get to his feet. Kyle got his first, good look at the blood running down the hound's side and he reached out and ran his hand over it. Bosley jerked away from the pain it caused and yelped.

"Sorry, Boz. I didn't realize you were hurt this bad. Let's get you out of here."

Even Buster stopped playing the bad cop when he saw how bad Bosley was hurt. He just walked alongside the hell hound as they moved to the back of the truck. Kyle let the tailgate down and Bosley climbed slowly up and into the bed and as he settled down, the springs on the truck groaned with agony and the back of the truck settled down on the rear tires.

"Damn. I'm glad I have those airbags installed in the rear suspension."

He reached in and started the engine and then flipped a switch and he could hear the compressor come on and start filling the airbags in the springs. In a few seconds the bed of the truck began to lift off the tires and pretty soon, he had the truck riding level again.

He picked up Buster and set him in the front of the truck and closed the door. Before leaving, he wanted to talk to the sheriff, who was standing near the back of the paramedic's unit, as they loaded Debbie in next to Farmer Smith. After they closed up the back of the unit, the three men stood there and watched as it pulled away and started back across the field.

"So, John, Cal, what the hell happened out here?"

The sheriff looked at him and all he could say was, "Monster attack."

"That's it? That's all you have to say? There are some nasty rumors going around town right now and no one knows what to think."

"Kyle. Now is not the time!" said the sheriff.

"Sorry, sheriff. And I'm dreadfully sorry about Debbie. But there seems to be something tearing away at this town and I think the townsfolk need to be told something."

The sheriff shot him a glance and turned to face him. Cal stepped in between the two to keep them apart.

"Look Kyle, we're not sure what we want to tell the townsfolk right now," said the deputy. "Yes, they need to be told something, but we need to be careful about when and how we put it out there."

"No," said the sheriff, "Manning's right. The town needs to know."

He turned and looked at Kyle and said, "Tomorrow, three o'clock in the high school gym. Get the word out. Now, get out of here and get Bosley to your place. As you said, Lita probably has something she can do for him."

Kyle nodded, turned and headed to his truck. As he was driving away, the last thing the sheriff and deputy saw and heard was Buster looking down, through the sliding glass window at Bosley in the bed of the truck and whimpering at the hell hound.

"You don't think this is going to cause a panic?" asked Cal.

"This is a town full of monsters. We need to let them know that there is a monster worse than any of them on the loose."

They walked over to the place where Bosley had fallen and where Debbie had been. They spent a few minutes looking around for any clues as to where the Boogerman had gone, but there was nothing.

They called the search off quickly, mostly because the sheriff wanted to head to the hospital and check on his baby and he definitely didn't want Cal out there by himself. The sheriff gave Cal a ride back to his truck that was in front of Debbie's house and then took off for the hospital.

~~~~

"Daddy, I don't know what to tell you."

"Tell me anything, sweetie. I have a meeting this afternoon with the entire town and I need to know what to tell them."

Debbie looked at her dad as he sat in the chair next to her hospital bed. She had never seen him look so vulnerable, so afraid. He dealt with monsters on a daily basis, but the return of the Boogerman was way beyond the everyday thing.

"I can tell you, I think he is one of the undead."

"You're sure about that?"

"No, I'm not sure! I was face-to-face with him, could see his eyes and I still couldn't see his face. When I jammed my fingers into his face, it felt like I was touching Death itself."

The sheriff picked up her hand and looked at it. The hospital had done way too good a job cleaning her up when she was brought in. There was no skin or meat under her fingernails.

"How's Farmer Smith?" she asked.

"He's pretty tore up, but the docs say he'll recover. I don't know what it is we're dealing with here, but anything that could take down a windigo is not something to be trifled with."

"You might want to send someone out to Farmer

Taylor's place and warn him. He's right next door, so he could become a target."

Sheriff John nodded and said, "He'll probably be at the meeting."

As he stood up, he leaned over and kissed her on the forehead.

"Ooo, sheriff. Kissing your deputy. What would people think?"

"I don't really care what people would think," he said smiling.

"Hey, you might also want to check on Bosley."

"Oh, no. I'm not going out there."

"C'mon daddy. He saved my life."

"I understand that and Bosley isn't the problem."

"Oh for crying out loud. Buster is just a little wiener dog right now."

"Yeah! A little wiener dog that terrifies a hell hound! That scares me!"

Debbie blew a raspberry at the sheriff as he was walking to the door and said, "Chicken!"

"You're damn right!"

Before leaving the hospital, he stopped to check on Farmer Smith. He was still in his windigo form, so they had to have two beds pushed together to contain him.

Truth be told, this scared the sheriff more than any demon dog. Any monster that could take down a windigo and a gargoyle was the thing of nightmares.

Chapter 7

~~

There is no escape

The meeting was going pretty much how Sheriff John figured it would. Lots of talking over each other, lots of scared people wondering what the sheriff was going to do and lots of yelling. Just another ordinary meeting of the townsfolk.

"Do you think we should think about leaving town?"

The sheriff looked at Terry, the green grocer.

"I don't know, Terry. That is completely up to you. I wouldn't tell any of you to stay if you didn't want to."

Jake Johnson stood up and yelled, "We are not going to run scared!"

There was quite a lot of agreement with that sentiment from the rest of the folks. Jake and Randy Johnson had been all over the hills where the Boogerman had last been seen and found no trace of him.

"I'm not asking you to run scared, Jake." said the sheriff. "But, a lot of the people here are not as young as they once were and if they need to clear out of town for awhile, until we find this demon and take care of him, then I don't think we should hold it against them."

"All I'm saying is that we're here to help you sheriff, and we're here to fight."

"I appreciate that. You and your brother have been a great help these past few days and I feel safer knowing you're helping."

Jake sat back down, but Terry was still standing.

"Something else, Terry?"

Terry looked around and took a deep breath.

"I am also appreciative of the Johnson boys and anyone else that is ready to stand and fight this monster. But, as the sheriff says, some of us are getting on in years and we wouldn't be much help in a fight. We would just get in the way."

He looked back at the sheriff and said, "I'm gonna close up the store for the time being and take Milly and go on vacation. I don't want to be thought of as a coward, but I also can't ask my sweetie to stay and fight this demon."

The sheriff stood up and looked him right in the eyes.

"Terry, I don't think you're a coward and would never begrudge a man wanting to protect the ones he loves by getting them out of harm's way. If I thought it would do any good, I'd ask you to take Debbie with you, but I know that ain't happening."

The rest of the room kind of chuckled at the

thought of the sheriff trying to get his daughter to leave town until the monster was dealt with. He'd have an easier time trying to contain Buster in full moon, demon-dog mode.

Terry sat back down and the sheriff could tell there was a growing sentiment in the room that some would be following his lead. He wasn't too upset by that either. The more people that left town meant the fewer people he had to worry about keeping safe.

"Alright," said the sheriff, "just to let you know where we stand. We, meaning the sheriff's department and the Johnson boys, have been all over those hills and we can't find any trace of this Boogerman. We know he's up there somewhere, but damned if we can find any clues."

He looked at Kyle and asked, "Any chance Buster can be of some help in trying to track him down?"

Kyle shrugged his shoulders and said, "He's not much of a tracking dog, sheriff. He's more of an attack dog, but only when it's full moon time and that's almost two weeks away."

"Hey sheriff," said Randy Johnson, "I thought you and Buster didn't see eye-to-eye."

There was a laugh that went through the crowd.

"Randy, at this moment in time, I'm willing to try anything, even using that mangy mutt if it will help."

The rest of the meeting went pretty quickly and it began to break up. Terry stopped by the sheriff and offered his hope that they could take care of this quickly.

"I hope so, Terry," said the sheriff, who then turned to the little old lady, using a walker. "Milly, you be safe and we look forward to having you come back. Nobody makes pumpkin muffins like you."

Milly looked up at him with a smile and said, "Sheriff, you catch this monster and you'll have pumpkin muffins for the rest of your life."

The sheriff laughed and patted his tummy.

"Yeah, that's just what I need."

"If I was two hundred years younger, John, I'd be staying here and tearing that Boogerman up by myself."

The sheriff reached out and put a hand on her shoulder and said, "I know you would, Milly."

He watched as Terry placed a hand on her shoulder and helped guide her toward the exit. He made a solemn promise to get this demon under control so good folks like the Oswalds could live in peace again.

~~~~

The headlights shone down the road, lighting the way through the forest. The Oswalds were ready to get out of town and they couldn't do it fast enough. Terry didn't really care for the route up highway 89 that cut through the forest and into the hills north of Prattville, but it was the fastest way north and on to North Platte, where their daughter lived with her husband and their three grandkids. If anything could raise Milly's spirits about leaving her home, it was seeing the grandbabies.

He called Connie to let her know they were coming and she was elated. Her parents hadn't been out of Prattville in over forty years and she was happy to have them coming. She found it strange though, papa wouldn't say why they were coming, just that they wanted to get away from Prattville for a little while.

Milly sat in the right hand seat and was doing a little knitting. She had a couple of booties finished for one of the babies and she had every intention of finishing one more pair during the three hour drive. Besides, it kept her mind off the darkness outside and the fact that they were driving through the forest the Boogerman was rumored to be running around in.

Terry hummed along with the Glen Miller tape he had in the stereo. Their old car had never even seen a CD and probably wouldn't know what to do with one. Earl had tried a couple of times to install a stereo for them that would connect to their smart phone, but they kept putting him off.

"We never go anywhere worth the time to hook it up, Earl."

That's all they ever told him.

"Pardon me boy, is that the Chattanooga choo-choo?" hummed Terry.

Coming over a rise about twenty minutes out of town, something flew across the road and smashed into their windshield. It was black and moving fast. It was just after nine at night, so it was dark outside the car, but still, when the headlights hit the object, they saw nothing, but a black shape.

Even though Terry wasn't known as the fastest driver in the world, they were still traveling fast enough for him to lose control and roll the car into the ditch. The car came to rest on its wheels, but it was clear that car was going nowhere ever again.

Terry was killed almost instantly, while Milly, still buckled into her seat, was knocked unconscious. When she regained consciousness she could feel the blood running down her face and into her eyes. As she tried to see what had happened, the blood gave her vision an evil, red glow. At least she thought it was the blood doing it. It might have been something else coming from deep inside her.

She looked over and saw Terry sitting next to her, but she knew by looking at him that he was dead. She could feel her rage beginning to grow inside her tiny body and she knew she was on the path to change and it would only take a few seconds.

She tried to unbuckle her seat belt, but she had

broken her right arm and didn't have the strength to undo it with her left hand.

She saw their cell phone sitting on the seat next to Terry and she reached for it and picked up. As she pushed the power button, she could feel herself beginning to lose consciousness again, so she knew she needed to hurry. Dialing 911, she waited for the emergency operator to come on.

As the phone rang, she looked up, through her blood covered eyes and saw a dark figure standing in front of the car. One of the headlights was still working and the light was shining directly on the demon, but it didn't light it up at all. It was as if it was a black hole in space, absorbing all light directed at it.

It started moving toward the side of the car where she was trapped and she tried even harder to undo the seat belt, but she was in full panic mode now and she couldn't press the release button.

Then she felt the fingers of the demon grab her by the throat and try to pull her out of the car.

"911. What is your emergency?"

All she could do was gargle helplessly as the demon tried again to pull her out of the car, but the seat belt held her firmly. The demon used one of its super long fingernails to cut through the belt and when it released, it pulled her through the window.

She dropped the phone on the way out of the car and the 911 operator could hear her scream. It wasn't the only thing she heard. The low, guttural growl she heard, sounded like Hell had opened up and spewed out all its anger.

Freed from her seat belt, Milly was able to change into her true form, that of a large vampire. Even though she stood barely four and a half feet tall as a human, she rose to seven feet tall as a vampire and she had a wingspan of almost eight feet.

The only problem was, she was still old and still weak with age and the car crash hadn't helped matters.

The demon still had her by the throat and threw her down on the ground. As it fell on top of her, getting in close enough for her to see eyes under the hood, she screamed and then raged at him. This monster had just killed the one man that didn't care if she was a vampire, still asking her to marry him.

She began to fight back with every ounce of strength she had and with the one weapon she still had. Clutched in her arthritic, old, left hand was just what she needed. Her hand came up with a fury and she drove the knitting needle right through the lower jaw of the demon and straight up into its head.

The demon rolled off her and screeched in pain as it clawed at the needle to pull it out. When it finally came loose, it looked at it and then tossed it away, turning its attention back to this old vampire that just hurt it.

She was trying to raise herself up, but with a broken right arm, she was still in grave trouble. She pushed herself up to her knees and let her wings spread to their full extent. She looked up at the demon with every bit of rage her old body could muster.

"Come here you spawn of Hell! I'm gonna rip every piece of meat off your bones!" she croaked at him through her pain.

As she went to stand up, the demon charged her and she brought her left hand up again, this time without a knitting needle. She only had one of those. But, what she lacked in needles she more than made up for in claws at the end of her fingers. She drove her fingers into the chest of the demon and was horrified to find it didn't even feel it when her claws sank all the way up to the second joint on her fingers.

The demon grabbed her again by the throat and she raged at him with all the fury she could gather from the depths of Hell. The demon screeched in her face and then screeched in pain as she pulled her fingers out of its body, bringing with it as much flesh and muscle as she could get her hands on.

This just further enraged the demon and he slashed at her face with his free hand, cutting most of the skin off her skull with his fingernails. Blood gushed out of her wounds and ran down over his hand that was holding her by the throat.

She still tried to fight, but she just didn't have the strength to take him on. Maybe when she was a couple hundred years younger she could have taken him, but now, she was nothing more than a puppet in the hands of this demon.

~~~~

The 911 operator was already on the line with the Prattville sheriff's department and she reached Cal, who was just about ready to head out for another quick loop around the town. Even he could hear the sounds of the battle through the phone and knew exactly what was happening.

When the operator told him where she had tracked the cell signal to he yelled thanks and hit the door running. Before he had even reached his truck, he was on the radio with Sheriff John telling him what was up. He raced north on highway 89, hitting speeds at well over one hundred miles per hour, lights and siren blazing.

The 911 operator came on the radio and said she was sending state police down from the north, but Cal yelled at her.

"Don't do that! They will be walking into a situation they know nothing about and it will only get them killed. Our department will handle this!"

"Deputy, I need to send someone. It sounds like a

horrific attack going on!"

Then Sheriff John broke in, "This is Sheriff John Dinkendorfer of the Prattville Sheriff's department. Who am I speaking to and where are you located?"

"This is Officer Mallory at the state police barracks in Teston."

"Officer Mallory. I want you to call Lieutenant Cartwright and tell him where you want to send those state troopers. When you have talked to him, you'll have your answer."

~~~~

Debbie was awakened by the sound of the siren going past the hospital and a cold chill ran through her blood. When she heard the second siren go by less than two minutes later, she recognized it as her father's truck.

She tried to push herself up from the bed and groaned in agony. She was still feeling the effects of the attack from the night before and her head was still a little woozy.

The night nurse heard her groan and came running in from the nurse's station.

"Just where do you think you're going, deputy?"

"I have to get up," said Debbie as she tried to stand up.

Her knees were not at all happy about that

decision and they decided to buckle to keep her from doing something they were not prepared to participate in. As she fell forward, two very large hands grabbed her and lifted her right back into bed.

These were two very large, very green hands and the arms they were attached to were hairy and about as big around as cannons. Maybe this was where the term "guns" came from.

As she was put back in the bed she looked up and said, "Kelly, you didn't need to change just for me."

Looking down at her, was the biggest, ugliest ogre anyone had ever seen. Her bloodshot, red eyes bore right through her. When she spoke, it was with the deepest voice that had ever rattled the windows of the hospital.

"The sheriff told me that under no circumstances were you to get out of this bed no sooner than tomorrow and only after the doctor says it's okay."

Debbie knew she was going nowhere, especially with Nurse Ogre looking after her, so she resigned herself to staying in bed. Not that her body would have been much use in any attempt at a great escape.

She watched as Kelly changed back from an ogre to a beautiful, young, blonde nurse with a warm smile.

"I've never understood that."

Nurse Kelly looked at her and asked, "Understood what?"

"How you pack all that ogreness into that beautiful, little body."

Kelly laughed as she tucked Debbie back into bed.

"It's magic," she leaned over and said, letting her eyes flare red one last time. "Now, stay in this bed, deputy or I'll have tell your daddy."

"Tattle-tale," said Debbie with pouty lips.

Kelly smiled and laughed as she turned and walked back to her station.

Chapter 8

~~

No more pumpkin muffins

Cal reached the wrecked car within ten minutes of receiving the call and he could tell the fight had been massive. There was still steam curling out from under the hood of the car and he could see there was one occupant in the driver's seat.

As he bailed out of his truck, he grabbed the rifle from the rack at the center of the dashboard and ran to the car. He bent down and felt his heart break when he saw the lifeless face of Terry Oswald. He looked across the front seat and saw the passenger door was still closed, but the window had been broken out and there was blood on the window frame.

As he walked around the back of the car, he kept the rifle up, not sure what he was going to find. He couldn't hear anything except for the very weak strains of Benny Goodman playing *Sing, Sing, Sing*. As he reached the other side of the car, he found Milly, still in her vampire form.

She was dead, the flesh from her body completely torn to pieces. Even her wings had been broken and ripped. The part that scared Cal more than anything was her missing head.

He felt his breath becoming ragged as he was trying to deal with the sight in front of him. He could hear a siren in the distance and knew it had to be the sheriff coming up the road. He looked around, checking the edge of the forest, knowing that this had just happened and the Boogerman probably hadn't gone very far. He might even be standing there in the darkness, watching the whole scene play out.

He keyed the mic on his shoulder and called out, "John."

"Yeah Cal, go ahead."

"You better prepare yourself. It's Terry and Milly."

There was no reply and Cal didn't really expect one. He knew the sheriff was probably fighting with his emotions as he drove toward the scene. The Oswalds didn't deserve to go out like this and the sheriff was going to be enraged when he saw it.

Less than a minute later, the sheriff's truck screeched to a halt and John jumped out of the front seat, running to the driver's side window of the car.

"No!" he yelled as he saw the body of Terry, still strapped into his seat.

He looked across and saw Cal about twenty yards away, near the trees and he moved around to the other side of the car. He ran to where Cal was standing and the deputy placed a hand on his chest and stopped him.

"There's nothing we can do for her."

The sheriff looked at his deputy and shook his head and then pushed past him. When he knelt down next to the body of the vampire, he reached down and took hold of one of her hands. It was as cold as ice, but being a vampire, that was the usual state for her. But, her heart had always been warm and that's all that mattered to the sheriff.

He looked up at the night sky and raged at the stars shining down. He stood up and pulled his Glock and started firing round after round into the tree line.

"Come out and show yourself, you piece of shit!"

After his magazine was empty, he felt a hand on his shoulder and it helped to calm him down. He looked at Cal and shook his head.

"Sorry, deputy."

"Don't be sorry. You're not doing anything I don't want to do myself."

Then Cal turned away and pulled out his cell phone and dialed.

"Yes, this Deputy Worhl. We need you to come to milepost 153 on 89. We have two bodies for you to pick up."

Then he dialed another number and waited.

"Hey Earl, Cal here. We need you to come out to milepost 153 on 89 and pick up a car … Yeah, we've had another attack. Bring the flatbed."

As he put the phone away, he looked down and

saw something glinting in the flashing lights of their trucks. He took a handkerchief from his pocket and bent down to pick up the object. The sheriff saw him picking something up and he leaned over to see what it was.

"Kind of a strange thing to find out here." said Cal.

The sheriff looked at it and then at Milly's body.

"Not really, Cal. It makes perfect sense," he said as they looked at the knitting needle.

It was covered with gore, meat and whatever else it had come in contact with.

"Bag that carefully. We need to find out where that needle has been."

Then he walked over to Milly's body and crouched down again. He lifted one hand and then the other and was surprised to find a large chunk of meat and guts clenched in the fingers of the vampire.

"Oh, we're gonna get you, you sonavabich."

Cal was getting a plastic baggie out of his truck to put the needle in and John called to him and told him to bring a bigger one for Milly's hand.

About twenty minutes later the coroner's van showed up and Earl was about five minutes behind them. There wasn't a whole lot of talking going on as the two from the coroner's office went about loading the two bodies up and then pulled off the road a few yards away and waited. The sheriff had told them they were not to drive back to town alone.

Earl just stood in the middle of the road, shaking his head at the sight of the car in the ditch. The anger was welling up inside him and he was having a hell of a time keeping it at bay.

"It just doesn't seem right," said Earl as he turned to the two officers.

"What's that?" asked the sheriff.

"These two people were just getting out of here, trying to get away from the danger and it seems like the danger came looking for them. Almost like this Boogerman is saying no one is leaving this town."

The sheriff thought about that for a moment and then said, "Cal, doesn't it seem strange to you that the demon took Clara and Milly's heads, but left Terry's?"

"Maybe they are trophies to him."

Earl said, "That could be. Killing Terry would have been no great feat, but Milly put up a fight."

"Maybe he's only interested in collecting monster heads," said the sheriff, "but will kill anyone else that happens to get in the way."

They stood back and let Earl get on with what he came there to do and in about thirty minutes, all four vehicles rolled away from the accident scene. Cal drove in front and the sheriff pulled up the rear.

The sheriff couldn't shake the feeling that they were being watched every inch of the way back to town.

Chapter 9
~~
Hospitals are for the dying

Debbie was dozing in the early morning hours, wondering when the doctor would come by and give her the okay to leave. She didn't like being cooped up in the room painted in white, with white sheets and pillow cases. It was driving her crazy.

She hadn't heard anything about what had been happening last night causing both Cal and her dad to go racing by with sirens blaring. She knew something had happened, but she couldn't get any answers from anyone.

Just after eight, as she shut her eyes to try to relax, she heard a quiet knock on the door frame. Opening her eyes, she saw Officer Jeffers standing there looking at her.

"Tom, what're you doing here?"

Tom walked into the room and stood by her bed.

"Well, I guess I could ask you the same thing."

"Oh, I just had a little run in with one of the monsters and took a bit of a beating. Nothing too serious though. I'm just waiting for the doctor to come by and let me out of here."

She looked up at him, thinking she was glad to

see him. She hadn't even talked to him since the other night after their date. Of course, that was not her fault. Being thumped on by the Boogerman will put a kink in anyone's plans. He had left a couple of voicemails and text messages on her phone. She just hadn't taken the time to return any of them, which was bad, because she really did like him.

"How about you? Why did you come over to Prattville?"

"Well, because I heard that you had been injured in some sort of battle and I wanted to make sure you were okay."

She smiled up at him just as the doctor walked in.

"I'm fine. Just a little bruised up, that's all," she said looking at Tom.

The doctor went around the other side of the bed and said, "I'll be the judge of that, deputy."

"Doc, all I want to hear from you is get out of your hospital!"

The doctor looked at her and shook his head.

"Young lady. You went toe-to-toe with a demon and got the short end of the stick. I'm sure you're hurt a lot more than you're letting on."

"I'm fine! I'll be even more fine when you let me out of this place!"

She looked up at Tom, hoping to get a little support from him, but Tom just put his hands up.

"If the doctor says you stay, you stay," he said.

"You're no help."

As the doctor started looking at her bruises and checking her arms where the demon had hit her, he clucked his tongue a few times. She didn't like the sound of that and wanted him to stop it. He pressed a finger against her ribs and that brought a short intake of breath.

Tom looked at the doctor and asked, "Did she get some broken ribs, too?"

"No, she just has a nasty bruise here and I knew it would remind her that she's human."

"Hey doc," said Debbie, "is your driver's license and insurance up to date on your car?"

The doctor reached over and picked up his clipboard and scribbled a few things on it and then walked to the end of the bed and looked at her.

"Get out of my hospital, deputy. Oh, and keep it to light duty for a few more days. You're going to be sore and won't be back to one hundred percent for awhile."

Then he turned and headed out the door and Tom stood there looking at her with a smile on his face.

"Hey, feel like some breakfast?" he asked.

"Sure, as soon as you leave this room and close the door so I can get out of bed and put my clothes on."

"Don't you have one of those nifty hospital gowns

on?"

"Yes, yes I do and it is a bit drafty in the back."

Tom laughed and headed for the door, saying, "I'll wait out by the nurse's station for you."

After he left, she got up and moved to the closet and found her uniform. It was a little dirty from the encounter with the Boogerman, but it was still wearable. And breakfast sounded like a great idea, now that she thought about it. The hospital food here was the same as hospital food all over the world. Their kitchen was never going to be awarded five stars.

It took a little work, but she was able to get the uniform on and buttoned up. Putting her boots on was a whole different story, though. She ended up opening the door and asking Kelly if she could come in and help her, but Kelly was assisting another patient and said she would be right there.

Tom decided he could help, now that Debbie was more suitably dressed and walked into the room and asked what he could do.

"I was just going to ask her to help me with lacing up my boots," said Debbie sheepishly.

"I can do that," said Tom as he dropped down to one knee in front of her and began pulling the laces tight and tying them up.

She looked down at him and he had his head down, watching what he was doing and she realized that he really was a nice guy. Maybe she needed to pay a little more attention to him.

After he finished tying the laces, he stood up and then held out his hand to help her up. She noticed his strong, but gentle grip.

"Off to breakfast?" he said.

"Sure, but let's stop at the department on the way."

"You bet," he said as he followed her out the door and out of the hospital. Her truck was still at her place, so she climbed into his patrol car and they drove the three blocks to the sheriff's department.

Walking into the department, she saw her dad sitting behind his desk and she could tell he hadn't slept in at least a day, probably more.

"You look terrible, sheriff."

John looked up as her and shook his head.

"I feel about as good as I look."

He looked at Tom and said, "Good morning, Officer Jeffers. Come to check on the deputy this morning?"

"Yes, sheriff, I did. I hadn't heard from her since our dinner and then heard she had been injured and I decided to come by and see what happened."

"I guess I should warn you," said the sheriff, "Debbie is notorious for not keeping in touch like she should."

"Daddy! Stop it!"

She sat down at her desk and Tom sat across from her.

She looked at the sheriff and asked, "So, what happened last night that obviously kept you from getting any sleep. I heard you and Cal both go blazing past the hospital."

John dropped his head and then said, "The Boogerman struck again last night."

"Oh no. What happened?"

"He got Terry and Milly."

"Oh my god!"

"About fifteen miles north of here. They were on their way out of town, leaving to get away from here for awhile."

It was Debbie's turn to drop her head and fight to keep from crying. Terry and Milly were two of the nicest people she had ever known and this stung like a knife through the heart.

"Is this Boogerman the reason you want to talk to Ms. Handley?" asked Tom.

Debbie looked up and nodded.

"You haven't heard from the Handleys, have you?"

"No, nothing yet, but I told Edna to have her call you if they do call in."

He looked across the desk at her and could see she was feeling quite depressed with the news.

"I'm guessing breakfast is off now and I

understand that."

She looked up and said, "No, no. I could use something to eat. I just might not be very good company this morning."

"I'll chance it."

He turned and looked at the sheriff and asked, "Sheriff, care to join us for breakfast?"

"No, you two go ahead. Mabel is out sick today and I sent our other deputy home for the day."

"Okay, some other time then."

John nodded as Debbie came around the desk and gave him a kiss on the cheek.

"When I'm finished with breakfast, I'll come back and relieve you so you can go home and get some sleep."

John sat back and nodded.

"That would be wonderful."

~~~~

Debbie was right when she said she wouldn't be very good company. Try as she might, she just couldn't brighten up after hearing of the deaths of Terry and Milly.

She told Tom about how Milly had been her teacher in the third grade and she was the one that had hauled her to the principal's office when she thumped on the schoolyard bully. She had felt like she was being marched to a firing squad, but Milly had just kept patting her on the shoulder as she walked her along.

She had told her how she had done wrong, but there was no shame in standing up to bullies. When Milly left her sitting outside the principal's office, she left her with a wink and smile.

Tom listened and didn't say much. He just wanted her to talk it out, knowing that it would do her more good than anything he could ever say.

After breakfast, she had him drive her to the house so she could pick up her truck and head back to the department. After she got out of his cruiser and before he backed up, she walked around and stuck her head in his window and kissed him.

"Why, deputy a kiss on our second date," he said with a smile.

"Hopefully," she said, "with more to come."

He smiled and put the car into Reverse and backed up and turned around.

She was grinning from ear-to-ear.

~~~~

"Daddy! I am NOT going to come live with you!"

"Sweetie, I think it would be best until we catch the Boogerman. We still don't know where he is, but he's out there somewhere. And it also seems that he has something against you."

"I never should have told you what he said."

The sheriff stood and looked at his daughter and just shook his head. How he had gotten such a pig-headed daughter was beyond him. She reminded him of ... well ... her mother.

Debbie felt a little bad for getting mad at her father for what he was saying. Even she knew it was foolish to go back to her house all alone, with the Boogerman still on the loose. With Bosley laid up and Farmer Smith still in the hospital, she didn't really have anyone that would be around if she got into trouble.

"Look," she said, "I'll come stay at your place, but only until Bosley is ready to go back on duty."

"That could be awhile. He was hurt pretty bad."

"Yes, but I'm sure he's ready to get as far away from Buster as he can."

Chapter 10

~~

Missing mom

Four nights passed since the attack on the Oswalds and there hadn't been any sign of the Boogerman in that time. People were starting to wonder if maybe he had decided to move on.

Sheriff John and the whole sheriff's department knew that was a fool's hope. They didn't expect this to end like it did twenty years ago.

Back then, after Cindy had been taken, the whole valley around the town had been searched and when she was found, the Boogerman just up and vanished. There was no reason the sheriff could see for that to happen. It just did.

One thing the sheriff had felt back then, was the Boogerman was young and inexperienced in whatever he was doing. Like he was an amateur or something. Like he was just learning to deal with being the monster that he was.

But the killing of the five monsters after she was found seemed like the demon was acting on pure rage, as if something had been taken from him and he was angry about it.

~~~~

Four nights of peace and quiet, with the town beginning to calm down.

The Oswalds had been laid to rest in one of the biggest funerals the town had seen in many years. Monsters of all kinds showed up and they all cried over the loss of their friends.

During the grave-side service, the monsters didn't hide who they truly were. Werewolves cried on the shoulders of demons, vampires consoled ogres. Burial day would have been a perfect day for some monster hunters to come to town. The sheriff's department was glad that none did.

Some would say the Oswalds would be missed because they were going to miss Milly's pumpkin muffins. The sheriff wasn't kidding when he said they were the best he had ever tasted. When the smell of those muffins wafted into the air around the small store she and Terry had owned for years, there were people ready to line up to get a box or two. Milly always made sure to hold back a dozen and had Terry walk them across the street to the sheriff's department and when he walked through the door with that white box, nobody smiled bigger than the sheriff.

Debbie grabbed a bag of her things and moved into her old room in her dad's house. He never did change anything in that room, leaving all her things exactly the way she left them when she went off to the Army.

As she walked into the room, she almost had to giggle at the posters of NightRanger and Blondie on the walls. As she set the bag down on a chair and sat down on her bed, she looked around and felt the memories starting to flood back. She could almost hear her mom downstairs in the kitchen, rattling pots and pans around, preparing dinner.

Dad would come walking in from work just after six and she would always race down the stairs to see what kind of monsters he had had to deal with that day. Most of the time there were no stories to tell. Sometimes he'd tell of arresting some lookie-loos and sticking them in the nonexistent cells in the basement for the night.

Her mother wasn't what you would call a real monster. She was one of those that was from out of town. Way out of town.

Her small spaceship had developed mechanical issues and crash landed just behind Farmer Smith's place. When the sheriff went to investigate, he found her standing next to her busted ship, fuming about how she was going to get off this dreadful planet. She was completely flabbergasted when the sheriff rolled up in his truck and got out and started talking to her like this was an every day thing.

She stood about six feet tall, almost as tall as him

and she had a very pale, blue skin that she was able to control to make it look more human-like when she needed to. Her sparkling blue eyes were as kind as anyone had ever seen. Oh, and she was beautiful. Being the top-notch law man that he was, that fact didn't escape his keen sense of observation.

After he contacted Earl to come and get her ship out of the field and hidden in his shop, he offered to take this new visitor to get something to eat. The rest is history, as they say.

It took less than four months for them to fall in love and get married and about a year later, Debbie was born. She didn't exhibit any of the traits of her mother, nor did she have any special abilities other than being stronger than an ox. She didn't even inherit any of the height gene from either of her parents.

One night, after she had gone to sleep, she could hear a commotion downstairs and crept to the top of the stairs to see what was happening. She could hear some angry talking, some from her mother, some from her father, but also some from another man's voice she'd never heard before.

As she crouched in the darkness, there was a flash and a sound that was like the laser guns you hear in the movies. She heard her mother scream and she raced downstairs to find her mother standing in the middle of the living room, trembling with fear. Her father was holding one of his weapons. There was no one else in the room.

"What happened?" she asked.

Her parents looked at her, terrified that she might have seen something.

"Nothing, sweetie." said her mom. "You father's gun just went off by accident."

She knew that was a load of bullcrap, but she didn't have any evidence to back up her suspicions. But, the gun her father was holding was unlike any gun she had ever seen before.

Her dad took her back upstairs and as they were climbing the stairs, she looked over and saw her mom was trying to keep from crying. After she went back to sleep, she was awoken in the early hours of the morning, by her mother sitting on the edge of her bed.

"Hey, sweetie, I'm going to have to go away for a little while."

"Where are you going, mommy?"

"I have to take a trip. But, your daddy is staying here and he will always be here for you."

"Can I go with you?"

"I wish you could, but where I'm going, I can't take you."

Then her mom leaned over and kissed her on the forehead and then they hugged. A few seconds later, her mom got up and left the room and that was the last time she ever saw her.

It wasn't until a few years later that her father told her about her mother. He told her that she had fled the planet because some bad people from her home had come looking for her and they would have killed her if she stayed here. She left to keep her family safe.

She found all this out after her run-in with Kenny Kline. Even though he was quite proud of his daughter taking down the schoolyard bully, her father had broken the news to her about her mother and that she needed to watch herself. She had so much extra strength she could do some serious damage if she wasn't careful.

She reached over and pulled a drawer out on her old desk. Right on top of the things in the drawer, was a framed photo of her and her mom and dad. She pulled the photo from the drawer and sat there looking at it.

That was over twenty years ago and she hadn't heard anything from her mother since. She still had no idea why her mother was the target of other aliens and she didn't think her father even knew.

She took the photo and set it up on the desk, so she could see it while she was there in the house.

A few minutes later she heard her dad come in downstairs and she got up and walked down to see how he was doing.

~~~~

For four nights, nothing happened. The peace and quiet of the small town had returned, though the townsfolk were still a bit on edge. They had started venturing out of their houses again, starting to build a little more courage in the face of the threat that loomed over them.

But, that peace and quiet was never going to last.

Just after two in the morning, the quiet of the night was shattered by a screech that was born on the wind. It was heard throughout the entire town and everyone knew what it was. Those that were still outside raced to their homes and locked the doors. Never, in the history of the world, had monsters ever been so afraid of another monster.

Sheriff John and Cal heard the screech, even though they were in different parts of town. Sheriff John had gone home for the night, but was still awake in his study. Debbie was asleep in her bedroom, still recovering from her injuries from the week before. He left the house as quietly as he could and didn't bother getting on the radio until after he was in his truck and pulling away from the house.

That didn't make any difference. Debbie had heard the screech and she had her own radio sitting right beside her bed. When she heard her father getting in contact with Cal, she crawled out of bed and began getting dressed even though it was still quite a painful experience. The best she could manage was a track suit and sneakers she had been wearing for a couple of days. It would have taken her at least thirty minutes to put on her uniform and boots.

Within a few minutes she was stepping down the stairs and out the front door and heading for her own truck.

She climbed into the front seat, but didn't start the engine. She just sat there listening to the other two on the radio, trying to decide what she was going to do. As she listened she heard the sheriff and Cal coordinating their movements through the northern part of the town.

They started in the southeast corner of that quadrant of the town and started working their way north and west. As they drove through the dark streets there was no sign of the demon and they began to wonder if maybe the wind had just been playing tricks on their minds.

The townsfolk could have answered that question for them. There was no way the wind had sent that cold chill through their bones, causing them to cower in fear in their homes. They knew the Boogerman was on the prowl and looking for its next target.

After about thirty minutes Cal called the sheriff and told him to meet him at the Morgan place.

"Did you find something?" asked the sheriff.

Debbie could hear Cal come back, "Yes, sheriff, but I don't want to go inside until I've got some backup."

She reached over and started the engine and pulled quietly out of the driveway and into the street. Flipping on her headlights, she rolled slowly down the street and then made the right turn that would take her to the far northwest corner of town and to the home of Mike and Judy Morgan.

She gripped the wheel tight and her knuckles went white with the pressure. She felt herself almost wanting to cry when she thought of Mike and Judy. They were both goblins, but both of them were sweet people, always looking for ways to lend a helping hand. They had both been teachers at the high school when she was a student there.

About five minutes later she rolled up in front of the Morgan house and parked behind her daddy's truck as it sat outside with its red and blue lights flashing. Cal's truck was parked in front of it and his lights on, too. The lights in the house were out, but she could see the glow from their flashlights moving through the house.

She reached over and flipped on her lights and then climbed out of the truck, moving to the back and opening the weapons vault. She reached in and pulled out two glowing pistols and then pushed the lid down on the vault.

She could see that her daddy and Cal had gone in through the front door of the house, so she decided to go around back. As she got to the back of the house she could hear what sounded like something moving through the rear of the house. She backed up, away from the door and into the shadows of a couple of trees. With her thumbs she flipped the safety switches off on her guns and then moved them behind her back so they couldn't be seen by somebody coming out the back door.

    Then she just waited.

    A few seconds later she heard Cal yell, "Stop right there!"

    She heard a crash and heard her father yell, "Watch out!"

    Debbie turned herself part way to the side so she could be in a sturdy firing position if she needed to fire. She kept her eyes on the back door and still she just waited.

    She heard one of the weapons from the other officers go off and saw the flash through the windows. There was a screech and another crash that sounded like some furniture being knocked over and then she heard her father yell, "He's heading out the back door!"

    Debbie was ready.

    Within a second the Boogerman came crashing through the back door and down the steps and she could see his red eyes hidden back, underneath his hood. She could hear the raspy breathing of a wild animal and this wild animal had been wounded.

As the Boogerman reached the bottom steps Debbie brought both pistols up and started firing. If there was one thing Debbie was good at, it was shooting with both hands. As her shots found their marks, the Boogerman screeched and charged her, but she just kept firing. She aimed a couple shots right between the blazing red eyes, but those shots missed and slammed into the back of the house.

Just as the Boogerman was about to reach her John appeared at the back door and fired his rifle knocking the Boogerman completely off his intended path. As the demon was thrown to the right, Debbie just kept firing, hitting it over and over again.

The demon decided it had seen enough and disappeared into the trees north of the house. Debbie went to try to follow him, but she was still a little sore and couldn't move as fast as she wanted to. Sheriff John came charging down the steps and Cal was right behind him and they caught up to her in just a couple of seconds.

"What the hell are you doing out here?" yelled the sheriff.

"Well, how about a thank you, sheriff?"

"A thank you?" he bellowed. "I should run you right back to the department right now and lock your ass up in a cell!"

They stood there looking at each other, neither one of them wanting to back down.

"I couldn't just lay there in bed, listening to you two on the radio and not come out here and help," she said.

"That is exactly what you should have done!"

Cal reached up and patted the sheriff on the shoulder and then turned around and started toward the back door. The sheriff looked at Debbie and then just shook his head and turned to follow his other deputy. Debbie turned and looked towards the woods. But she knew the demon had disappeared into the night and there was no going after him.

She turned and headed toward the house and climbed the steps to the back door. Stepping through the door the smell of fresh blood assaulted her senses and she knew what she was going to find. She was pretty sure it was going to be the same thing she saw at Clara's house and she wasn't sure if she was up for it.

She walked through the kitchen and into the living room and was horrified at the sight. The bodies of Mike and Judy were in the middle of the room and looked like they had been torn to pieces.

Both heads had been separated from their bodies, but this time, they were left behind. Probably because the demon was interrupted in his attack.

Debbie began to feel nauseous and stepped through the living room and out onto the front porch. After a few minutes, she felt a presence beside her.

"I'm sorry. I know you want me to stay out of this, but just like you, I am a law enforcement officer."

"I know," said her dad. "I'm just worried about you getting hurt again."

She turned and looked at him.

"I'm not the only one that's been hurt. This Boogerman hasn't just killed people. He's injured just as many. You for example."

Her dad just shook his head.

"Look," she said, "I understand. But, I can't just sit on the sidelines on this one. The people of this town are my friends. Cindy was also a target. I need to see this finished, just like you do."

The sheriff reached out and squeezed her shoulder and nodded.

"Why don't you go home. We've already called Chester and he's on his way. I doubt we'll see anything of the Boogerman again tonight. Go get some rest."

She reached up and patted his hand and then stepped down off the porch and headed for her truck. Climbing in, she started the engine and looked at her dad through the dirty windshield. Then she backed up and headed back to the house.

All the way back to her dad's place she could feel

something clawing at the back of her mind, trying to work its way to the top of her thoughts. There was something about this case that she felt she should be seeing.

She crawled back into bed and laid there, looking up at the ceiling. She knew the chances of her getting any sleep were pretty much shot.

After trying for close to an hour, she looked at the clock and saw that it was just after four in the morning.

Kicking off the blankets, she headed into the bathroom to take a shower. It still hurt to move around, but she did the best she could.

After letting the water wake her up fully, she got dressed in her uniform, taking about ten times longer to do it than usual.

"You're an idiot for getting out of bed. You're not ready for this."

She wanted to tell the small voice in her head to shut the hell up, but she knew it was right. If she had a lick of sense she would go back to bed and stay there, sleep or no sleep.

She walked down the stairs and out the front door. She stopped on the porch and looked around. The sun was just beginning to brighten the sky in the east and it would be up in less than an hour.

As she drove through the quiet town, she could see the lights were on in the diner and she realized she was a bit hungry, so she pulled into one of the diagonal parking spaces out front.

Walking through the doors, she looked around and saw the usual crowd. Well, not really a crowd. There were three customers, one waitress and the cook in the back. With her there were six people in the whole place.

Carrie walked over as she took a seat in a booth.

"Mornin' Debbie," she said as she set a menu down in front of the deputy.

"Good morning, Carrie. Oh, I don't need the menu. Just get me some scrambled eggs, hash browns and sausage, with some coffee."

Carrie wrote down the order and picked up the menu and turned to walk away, but then turned back.

"You're really going to make me ask, aren't you?"

"Ask what?"

"About what happened a few hours ago. We all know something happened."

Debbie looked around and could see everyone was looking at her. There was a lot of fear in all of those tired, old eyes. She could feel her heart breaking thinking about the terror that could cause a group of monsters to tremble in fear.

"The Morgans were attacked this morning." she said quietly as she looked down at the table.

"Mike and Judy?" gasped Carrie.

Debbie just nodded her head, not wanting to look

anyone in the eyes.

She heard Carrie turn and walk away and as she watched her head for the kitchen, she could see the waitress' shoulders were bobbing up and down as she cried.

"Why did I even come in here?" she thought to herself.

As she waited for her breakfast, she looked around and could see everyone else was lost in their own thoughts. A couple more early risers came in the door and sat down near the other diners and it didn't take long for them to get the news.

After about ten minutes, Carrie brought her meal back and Debbie could see the redness in her eyes.

"I'm so sorry, Carrie. I wish I never had to tell you that."

"Is this ever going to end?" asked the waitress weakly.

Debbie looked up at her, pausing from putting ketchup on her hash browns.

"Just as the sky is blue, I promise you this will end."

Carrie looked out the window, at the cloudy skies.

"The skies look pretty gloomy to me today." she said as she turned and headed to take care of the other customers.

Debbie went ahead and ate her breakfast, but it

just didn't have the taste it usually did. Carrie came back a couple times to refill her cup, but didn't say anything.

A few minutes later, as she was finishing up, Carrie walked up with the check and set it down.

"This Boogerman must really hate teachers."

Debbie looked up at her and asked, "What do you mean?"

"Well, Clara, Mike, Judy, Terry and Milly were all retired teachers. So was Bill. I think even Farmer Smith used to be a teacher, but I'm not sure."

The deputy sat there for a second as the fog in her brain lifted and that thought that had been scratching at the back of her mind came roaring to the front.

"Oh my god!" she said as she jumped up.

She pulled a twenty from her wallet and handed it to Carrie as she raced out the door. Jumping in her truck, she backed out onto the street and flipped on her lights and took off.

Racing back to the Morgan house, she screeched to a stop, just as a couple of attendants were loading the two bodies into the back of the van.

Her dad came down the steps, followed by Cal and Chester.

"They were all teachers, daddy!"

"What?"

"All of the dead, were teachers. Even Bill and Farmer Smith, who I think was a substitute for a little while. Terry wasn't a monster, but he was a teacher."

The sheriff looked like he had just been gut kicked. He turned and looked at Cal.

"Can you take care of securing this place?"

"Sure thing, John."

He turned back to Debbie and started walking her down the sidewalk, toward their trucks.

"Back to the department, now," he said as he sent her to her truck and split off toward his truck.

Chapter 11
~~
Getting a better idea

Debbie sat behind her desk, which was across from her dad's. She was just about to say something when Mabel came walking in.

"Good morning sheriff, deputy."

"Mornin' Mabel," said the sheriff.

"So, it appears we have a demon that has taken a disliking toward teachers," said John, looking back at Debbie

"But, they were all retired," said Debbie, turning the conversation back to important matters.

"Who was retired?" asked Mabel as she set some papers down in front of the sheriff.

"All the victims of the Boogerman. Last night he got the Morgans. All the victims appear to have been teachers at some point."

"Oh dear," said Mabel. "I guess I should hope you catch him soon."

The sheriff looked at her and the light went on in his eyes.

"That's right. You were a teacher before coming to this department."

"Well," said Debbie, "obviously we need to look at what happened twenty years ago. Were any of those killed teachers?"

"What we need to look at is," said the sheriff, "who did the teachers come in contact with back then, that they all have in common."

"Sheriff," said Mabel, "this is a small town. We only have two schools and every teacher in both schools would have been part of every single student's life."

Debbie said, "What we need to look at is, who did the teachers make so mad that they would want to kill them now? If he really is targeting teachers, then something happened a long time ago and this demon hasn't forgotten it."

"Another thing we need to look at," said the sheriff, "is what teachers from back then are still around? This was twenty years ago, so a few may have moved away, some may have died and some may still be teaching."

"I'll call Benjamin at the school board office. He should be able to get a list like that together."

"Thanks Mabel." said the sheriff.

Debbie stood up and started to get ready to leave. The sheriff looked at her, wondering where she was going.

"I'm heading back to my place to get my yearbooks from those years. I don't know if the answer is in there, but it might be a place to start."

John stood up and said, "I'm coming with you."

"No, you're not," said Debbie. "I can take care of this myself. Besides, I'm going there, grabbing the yearbooks and coming straight back to town. The Boogerman doesn't attack in the daytime."

"He attacked me and Bill in the daytime."

"He attacked you as the sun was going down. It was already getting dark."

"I'd still feel better if I was going with you and I am your boss, you know."

"You're also my daddy," smiled Debbie. "I'll be fine. I'll be back here in less than thirty minutes."

The sheriff settled back in his chair and watched as she walked out the door.

"That is one willful child." he muttered under his breath.

Without even looking up from her paperwork, Mabel said, "Yes, I wonder where she got that from."

He looked at her with a bit of sneer, "Blah blah blah."

"Watch it, young man. I was your teacher at one time if I remember correctly. I'm sure you'd hate for me to start talking with Debbie about those days."

"Oooo. Blackmail. There are days when you surprise even me, Mabel."

~~~~

Debbie unlocked the front door to her house and

stepped inside. The place was quiet and a little stuffy. She hadn't been there for about five days now and it had been closed up tight.

She walked down the hallway to her bedroom and pulled open the closet door. On the floor, on one side of the closet, was a footlocker with a small padlock on it. She dropped down to her knees in front of it and opened the lock and set it aside.

Lifting the lid, she saw the mementos of a past life. A life stretching back almost thirty years. Her mother had taught her to remember the things happening around her, saying that there would come a day when she would want to look back and remember those events fondly.

There were old composition books, full of creative writing stories, back at a time when she thought being a writer would be her life. There were old report cards, attesting to the fact she had been an average student.

Pushed up against one side were three yearbooks, two for high school and one for primary school. She lifted the books from the foot locker and closed the lid and locked it back up. Picking up the yearbooks, she headed back down the hallway to the living room.

Walking into the kitchen, she decided she could stand to have a cup of coffee and began getting the pot ready to brew up a cup. After filling the water in the coffee maker, she sat at the small kitchen table, thumbing through the books.

As she started looking at the black and white photos of her friends, she had to laugh. There were the assorted faces with braces, eyes behind glasses and the usual rebels with the Mohawk haircuts and James Dean sneers.

Just about the time she thought the coffee maker would start sending forth its magical brew, a cold chill ran up her spine, causing all the hairs on the back of her neck to stand up. She jumped up from the chair, knocking it over backwards with a crash.

Looking around she knew there was no one there, except for her. But she couldn't shake the feeling of danger, so she reached over and flipped the power switch off on the coffee maker and headed for the door.

"I can get coffee at the diner or in the office."

After locking the door, she almost ran back to her truck and quickly locked herself inside before starting the engine. As she twisted the key in the ignition, she looked around, but didn't see anything.

"Outstanding Debbie. You're jumping at shadows now."

Slipping the truck into gear, she turned it around and headed out of the driveway and back to town. The whole way back was quite uneventful, but that didn't stop her from keeping an eye in the rear view mirror, halfway expecting to see some dark shape following her down the road.

It only took about ten minutes to get back to the office and when she walked in, carrying the yearbooks, she saw that the Johnson boys had joined her dad.

As she sat down behind her desk and started looking at the yearbooks, she realized that all talk had ceased. When she looked up she was met with four sets of eyes looking back at her.

"What?"

"Don't say what." said the sheriff. "What happened?"

"Nothing."

"Don't give us that crap, Debbie," said Jake. "I can see it wrapping itself all around you. Something happened back at your place."

She sat back and took a deep breath, calming her nerves. Then she told them about the cold chill and feeling that something had been watching her.

They all sat and looked at her. Mabel walked over with a cup of coffee and set it down.

"Thanks, Mabel." she said very softly.

Mabel patted her on the shoulder and turned back to her own desk.

"Well, that pretty much makes up our minds on where to start." said Randy.

Hearing Debbie's story, the Johnson boys decided her house was a good place to start. They decided it was going to be up to them to rid the town of this demon.

Randy and Jake Johnson were two of the roughest, toughest boys in the entire area. They had grown up working their family's ranch just south of town, working among the cattle since the time they were able to walk. Being twins, they started walking early and within a day of each other.

Being ogres meant they were capable almost from the time they got out of diapers. Besides their mother and father, there was only one person that scared them at all and that wasn't Debbie or the sheriff. It was their sister, Kelly, now a nurse at the hospital.

Debbie looked at those two boys and was quite happy that she never had to deal with them in a professional capacity. Though their strength and courage were legendary, so were their hearts. There was no one more willing to wade into a fight and stop it or help a person in need than those two boys.

As they were getting ready to leave the sheriff's office and head to her place, she stood in front of them and craned her neck to look up at them.

"You boys be careful out there. Hospital don't have no beds big enough for either one of you. Besides, if you get hurt, you'll be under the care of your sister."

They looked at each other and there was an unspoken agreement that went between them that, short of losing a limb, they could never place themselves in a position to having Kelly give them sponge baths.

They both looked down at the deputy and said, "Yes, ma'am."

They turned and walked out the door and she returned to her desk. Her dad was looking at her over his glasses.

"What?' she asked.

The sheriff leaned back in his chair and folded his hands across his tummy.

"I just hope those two aren't walking into something that even they can't handle."

"Sheriff, I didn't even want them to go."

"I know, but when you walked in here, we could all tell that you had seen or felt something at your place. You definitely weren't going to hide it from them."

She looked down at her desk and said softly, "I hope it was nothing. I hope I was just being a scaredy cat over a scratching at the windows."

"I hope so, too."

Chapter 12
~~
Even the ogres trembled

As Jake parked the truck in the driveway beside Debbie's house, they sat there for a moment. It was just after mid-day and there was a slight breeze blowing.

Randy rolled down his window and took a deep breath. He closed his eyes and started rifling through the catalog of smells in his mind, seeing if there was something there that shouldn't be.

Jake looked over at him after a few seconds.

"Anything?"

Randy opened his eyes and shook his head.

"The only thing I can smell is Taylor's hogs and they are pretty ripe today."

"Maybe Debbie's just runnin' scared from the thought of the Boogerman."

Randy looked at his brother and shook his head.

"The deputy don't got no scared in her little body. If she say she feel something, she feel something."

Jake looked back through the windshield, toward the trees a couple hundred yards behind the house.

"Ready to take a walk in the woods, brother?" asked Jake.

"Absolutely."

They both climbed out of the truck and then started undressing, stripping down to their underwear. Then each one of them stood tall, closed their eyes and let the change happen. Their breathing became rougher and deeper. Their bodies began to swell and turn green. Their arms grew to the size of tree trunks and their fists were as big as some of Farmer Taylor's hogs.

When the change was complete, they didn't stand six five anymore. They were both pretty close to eight feet tall and as wide as the truck they had arrived in.

They closed the doors to the truck and reached into the bed and pulled out their weapons. The weapon of choice for an ogre is a club about as thick as a telephone pole at the business end, with nasty, rusty spikes coming out of the head.

They wrapped their meathooks around the handles of those clubs and swung them around like they were badminton rackets. Then they nodded at each other and turned, walked past Debbie's house and toward the woods in the distance.

The Boogerman best be running if he knows what's good for him.

~~~~

Deep in a cave, about halfway up the mountain, the Boogerman moved around in the darkness. There was very little light shining from the entrance to the cave, but he didn't need any extra light to be able to see his way around. His was a world of darkness and this is where he was most comfortable. His eyes saw much better in the dark than in the light of mid-day.

As he moved slowly around the cave, he stopped at poles that had been driven into the cave floor. Each pole had a couple letters crudely scratched into it. CJ on one, MO on another. Two others had the letters MM and JM. There were six others arranged with them in a semi-circle, each with their own letters.

There were three poles sitting in the middle of the half circle, with the letters JD, DD and CL. These were placed in such a way that they looked like they were the most important of all the poles.

But, letters weren't the only things that adorned these poles. Sitting atop two of them, were heads. Gruesome, bloody, torn up heads.

On top of the pole with the letters CJ was the head of a gargoyle and atop the pole with the letters MO, the head of a female vampire.

The Boogerman stepped in front of the head of Clara Jensen and caressed the top of the skull. He laughed way down deep inside his evil chest as he slid sideways and in front of the vampire skull.

Milly Oswald had put up one hell of a fight and he looked at the head. Then he reached out and slashed at it with his long fingernails, ripping some skin from the skull.

He could still feel the pain between his ribs where she had removed a good chunk of his dead flesh. Pain was something he could still feel, but it took quite a lot to really hurt him.

"I should have taken your husband's head, too, but he weren't no monster. No thrill in taking his head."

He looked at the two poles set aside for the Morgans and he could feel his anger building. Another minute or two and he would have made his escape from their dark house with their heads. If it hadn't been for that deputy showing up when he did, he would have gotten away. Maybe he'd have to add another pole just for the deputy's head.

He moved away from the poles and toward the entrance to the cave. Looking out into the light that waited beyond the confines of the cave, he wasn't in any hurry to venture out. Night time was coming in a couple of hours and he would go out again and see if he could add to his collection of heads.

As he stood there near the entrance to the cave, he caught a whiff of something on the breeze. He knew the smell instantly and he didn't like it. If there was one thing he was even slightly afraid of, it was an ogre. Ogres were brutish, usually pretty stupid and only had one thing on their pea-sized brains and that was to smash anything that got in their way. If he had his way, he'd not tangle with an ogre anytime soon.

Maybe he wasn't going to have a choice.

He slunk back into the darkness of the cave and sat down on his haunches against the back wall. If the ogre was going to find him, he was going to have to look for him. He wasn't going to make it easy for him.

He looked over at the poles and then laughed to himself, thinking he just might need to add a new pole to his collection. One sturdy enough to hold an ogre head.

~~~~

Randy and Jake had been walking through the woods for a little over an hour and they knew that darkness was less than an hour away. Randy was starting to think it was time to head back, knowing that it would be dark before they got back to the truck.

"Maybe it's time to go back."

Jake looked at him and shook his head.

"We're staying out here. At least for another hour or two."

"Do you think it's safe?"

Jake looked at his brother and grinned with his dirty, yellow teeth.

"You're not afraid of the dark, are you?"

"Not afraid of nothing. Just can't see when it gets

dark."

"Well, I want to stay out here. You can head back if you like. Just don't take the truck and leave me to walk."

"If you stay, I stay."

Jake nodded and said, "Good. I just want to check one more thing before we leave."

"What that?"

"You remember that cave we used to hide in when mom and pop got mad at us?"

"Uh huh, I remember."

"It's just up the hill a little ways. I think we should check it out."

Randy didn't really care for the idea, but he nodded and they started heading up the hill.

Jake said, "If we don't find anything there, we go back and I"ll buy dinner tonight."

"Deal."

It took them about forty minutes to reach the cave and by then the sun had set below the mountains to the west. Though it was still light enough to see outside, inside it was black as a moonless, midnight sky. They both stood at the entrance and looked at the empty void in front of them. They both had the same thought, at the same time.

Why didn't we bring some flashlights?

Jake moved into the entrance and started back, into the cool darkness. Randy followed right behind him. Both of them had to duck down to keep from banging their heads on the roof of the cave and they had to turn a little sideways to keep from getting their shoulders wedged up against the walls.

After about ten feet, they came to a chamber, one that they remembered quite well from their days of hiding out there. There was almost a complete lack of light in the cave and Randy was correct when he said he couldn't see well in the dark. His brother had better night vision than him, so he let him lead the way.

He bumped into the back of Jake, who had come to a full stop in the middle of the cave.

"What's up, brother?"

"You don't want to know, bro. It ain't good."

Jake was looking around in the darkness, but there was enough glow from the entrance for him to make out the poles and the two heads that were perched on two of them.

"We found Clara and Milly's heads." he said.

Randy moved around his brother and squinted into the dim light. It took him a few seconds, but his eyes began to focus and he was able to see what had brought his brother to a stop. Two heads sitting on top of two bloody poles.

He backed up away from the sight and felt his leg brush up against something that felt like cloth. He whirled around just in time to see two red eyes flash and come straight at him.

"You demon son of a bitch!" he roared as he brought his left fist up to grab the Boogerman by the throat.

Jake heard his brother yell and turned to see the demon avoid his brother's attempt to grab him and drove right up into his face. Jake moved across the cave to try to help his brother and he saw the demon slash at Randy with his long claw-like fingernails.

Randy roared in pain as he felt a good chunk of his face get ripped off and he backed away. The demon kept advancing toward him and was not paying any attention to Jake.

Jake swung his club and completely missed the head of the demon, slamming the head of his club into the wall of the cave. The whole mountain shook when he made contact.

The demon lunged again and slashed at Randy's chest, tearing even more meat from his bones. Randy stumbled backward, falling against the poles and snapping a couple of them. Milly's head went flying through the air, bouncing on the ground and toward the entrance of the cave.

The Boogerman saw one of his treasures had been dislodged and it sent him into an even higher state of rage than he already felt. He dropped on top of Randy and started slashing away at the downed ogre.

He really should have been paying attention to

the other one. Jake wound up like a major league baseball player and swung his club and connected like he was trying to drive a fastball out of the park. He felt the spikes at the end of the club embed into the head of the demon and cause him to screech in pain.

The Boogerman flew off Randy and slammed up against the side wall of the cave. He saw Jake coming toward him, getting ready to swing the club again and he decided he needed to get out of there, instead of fighting two ogres. Besides, he had done his damage to one. The one that had desecrated his memorial to his evil rampage.

He screeched at Jake and ducked below the swinging club. He slashed at Jake's face, connecting and cutting Jake across the nose and eyes. This just infuriated Jake even more and he swung again. The demon dodged the swing again and slithered toward the entrance. On his way out of the cave, he snatched Milly's skull in his bony hand and disappeared out into the woods.

Jake chased after him, but when he got to the entrance, he couldn't see anything. He had blood running down his face and into his eyes and he could taste his own blood on his lips. He raged at the darkness, lifting his club to the sky, challenging the demon to come back and face him.

All he heard was a whole lot of nothing.

Then, he heard the raspy breathing of his brother behind him and he turned and headed back into the cave. Randy was not in very good shape and Jake knew he needed to get him to the hospital. But, the truck was almost two hours away and in the dark and with his own injuries, it would take even longer.

Then, thinking for a moment, he realized they were directly north of the town and only a couple of miles from the sheriff's department and the hospital. Much as he didn't like the idea, he needed to get his brother to the hospital and hope like hell tonight was their sister's night off. Facing Debbie was going to be bad enough. Facing Kelly would be a fate worse than facing the devil himself.

He reached down and ran his hands over the shoulder of his brother.

"Is there any possible way for you to get up and walk?"

Randy breathed out slowly and then said, "Can if you help."

"Hey, I'm your brother. I just don't think I can carry you."

He saw Randy start to struggle and stand up and he stood up to help him. He took Randy's arm and lifted it over his head and put it on his shoulder. Randy gripped his brother's shoulder tight and fought to keep himself awake.

Randy picked up his club and they moved

sideways through the cave tunnel and out into the night. He turned them to the right and started heading south, down the mountain. With any luck, they would reach the hospital in less than an hour.

Jake was a little afraid that the demon would realize how vulnerable they were with their injuries and decide to attack them as they walked down the mountain. He kept his head up and on a swivel. Even though he had blood streaming into his eyes, he was able to see well enough to know they weren't being followed.

About forty-five minutes later, the two of them staggered into the hospital lobby and the night nurse screamed.

"Doctor White, to the front lobby, stat!" she yelled into the microphone.

Then she ran around the counter to the two brothers, who were still ogres and helped get Randy to a gurney. As they got him laid down as best they could, the doctor came running from the back of the hospital.

He was followed closely by a cute, young, blond nurse.

Jake saw her and muttered to himself, "Oh good lord."

Randy was laying on the gurney, his arms and legs almost dangling to the floor, because the gurney wasn't made for someone as big as him. As the lobby nurse began helping the doctor push the gurney back to emergency, Kelly turned and looked at Jake and saw he was about ready to pass out.

She immediately changed and was able to help hold him up as she walked him back to the emergency rooms. She got him onto the table, with the same problem his brother had. The operating room table wasn't nearly big enough to hold him.

Kelly got him on the table as best she could and then rolled over a smaller table and lowered it until it was the same height as the operating table. She lifted her brother's legs up and set them on the new table, to make him as comfortable as possible.

As she began to wipe away the blood on his face and get him cleaned up as best she could she looked down at him and shook her head.

"Care to tell me what it was that you went and did this evening?"

"We found him, sis."

"Well, obviously you found him. And from the looks of things, he was a little bit more than you and Randy could handle."

Jake just laid there, taking the verbal chastisement from his sister, knowing full well that he deserved it.

"You need to get a hold of the sheriff and deputy and get them over here."

"Hold still for a minute, while I finish cleaning you up and closing these wounds and then I'll take care of getting in touch with them."

She continued working on him, stitching up the slashes in his face and after she was finished, he changed back into his human form. As she walked over to a closet to get a sheet, she changed back into her own human form. Draping the sheet over her brother, she turned and walked out the door, heading for the phone on the counter.

It took less than three minutes for the sheriff and deputy to come storming into the operating room and when Debbie saw Jake laying there, she went straight to him, leaned over and looked him in the eyes.

"Did I not tell you to be careful before you went out there?"

"Sorry, Deputy Debbie, but he came out of nowhere and attacked us."

Sheriff John walked up on the other side of the operating table and looked down at him and just shook his head.

"Where did this happen?"

"There is a cave about two miles directly north of here, about halfway up the mountain. That's where we found him."

Debbie looked at her dad and said, "I know that cave."

Her dad looked at her and then said, "We need to see who we can call on to go with us up there."

"Sheriff," said Jake, "it isn't a pretty sight up there.

Maybe leave Debbie down here."

Debbie looked at Jake and then at her father and said, "Ain't no one leaving me anywhere."

The two of them walked out of the operating room and over to the next room and looked in. They could see the doctor and the other nurse still working on Randy. Randy was still in his ogre form because he knew that if he changed back into his human form at that moment he would probably die from his injuries. Staying in his ogre form he was still strong enough to stay alive.

Kelly came out of the operating room behind them and she looked in the room at her other brother and Debbie could see she was fighting to hold the tears back. She reached out and put a hand on the nurse's shoulder.

"Is this ever going to end?" asked Kelly softly.

"Oh, it's definitely going to end." said the sheriff.

She turned and looked at him and said, "You stop that son of a bitch. Do it for Randy and Jake."

The Sheriff cocked his head and then said, "And for Clara and Terry and Milly and Mike and Judy."

Kelly dropped her head and then nodded, realizing that her brothers were still alive, while others had already lost their lives.

"Sorry, sheriff."

Sheriff John reached out and patted her on the shoulder.

"Don't be sorry. Now, get in there and help your brother."

Kelly wiped her eyes and then turned and walked into the operating room and began doing whatever she could to help save her brother's life.

"Hey sis." coughed out Randy.

She looked at him as he rolled his head towards her and he smiled.

"Don't you *hey sis* me. When we get finished patching you up and putting you back together, I'm gonna tear you to pieces."

They were both surprised to hear the doctor laughed a little bit and then he looked up from where he was stitching away at Randy's wounds and said, "Are you sure you want me to save you Randy? Sounds to me like you might be better off dying."

"Yeah," laughed Randy, "between her and our mom and pop, I'm not sure who's going to be worse."

As they continued working on the two brothers, the sheriff and deputy turned and headed out of the hospital and back to the department.

"Who are we going to call?" asked Debbie as she sat down at her desk.

John took a deep breath and then let it out slowly.

"I think it's about time to call an old friend."

Debbie looked at him, wondering who he was talking about. Then she sat back and the light went on in her head.

"You're not talking about Dean, are you?"

"That's exactly who I'm talking about."

Debbie shook her head and bit her lip.

"You don't like that idea?" asked the sheriff.

"No, sheriff, I don't. When he left here, he took a good portion of what would have made this department great with him."

"He only took himself!"

"Exactly!" she exclaimed. "He probably could have stopped this whole thing with one encounter with the Boogerman."

"Well, maybe so, but he had to do what was right for him. Moving to Teston was the right thing for him."

"I think he could have made just as nice a life here and his new wife could have moved here."

"She didn't want to."

Debbie was just about to say something when the front door to the department opened and a man walked in. He was dressed in a black suit, a white shirt with black tie and was wearing dark sunglasses. The sunglasses were a nice touch, seeing as how it was ten at night and quite dark outside.

The sheriff looked up from his desk and laughed when he saw him.

"Could you be any more obvious?"

The man looked at him, not even coming close to breaking a smile, while Debbie giggled in the background.

"You find this amusing, deputy?" said the man looking at her.

"Yes, I find you quite amusing, G-man."

He looked at her long and hard for a few seconds. She couldn't tell anything about his eyes because he still had the glasses on, but she was quite sure his glare was boring right through her.

"Hey, government man, over here." said the sheriff.

Debbie giggled again as the G-man turned back to the sheriff.

"Sheriff Dinkendorfer, my name is Agent Smith."

"Of course it is," laughed the sheriff.

The agent took a deep breath and let it out slowly. He was wondering why he always got sent to deal with the small town cops in situations like this, when what he really wanted to do was bust major crime rings in the big cities around the country. Now that was the excitement he wanted.

"I have been sent by headquarters to ..."

"May I see some ID?"

"Excuse me?"

"I'd like to see some ID," said the sheriff. "You say you're from headquarters, but haven't said HQ of what. FBI? CIA? Sanitation?"

Debbie busted out laughing at that last one. She knew her dad had no love for the feds, especially when they came to town and tried to tell him how to do his job with the locals.

Smith stood up a little straighter and reached into his breast pocket and pulled out a wallet and opened and showed it to the sheriff.

"Okay," said the sheriff. "Homeland Security. Forgive me for being so rude, but we had a guy in here last month from the Department of the Doughnut Hole Specifications and he was a real horse's ass."

Smith put his wallet away and then leaned over the sheriff's desk, placing both hands on the edge, trying to look menacing. Debbie just shook her head, knowing full well that Agent Smith was dangerously close to getting the full Sheriff John treatment.

"I have been sent down here by Washington to look into this little problem you've been having and to take control of it if I deem necessary."

The sheriff looked up at him and then slowly rose out of his seat. It was then that Smith began to realize just how large a man the sheriff really was. When the sheriff stood up fully, the agent stood up and backed away from the desk. The sheriff stood at least six inches taller than him and outweighed him by at least eighty pounds.

The sheriff leaned forward and placed two very large fists on his desk and looked Agent Smith directly in the eyes. Or directly in the sunglasses.

"Now, let me be perfectly clear here, so there is no misunderstanding," began the sheriff. "I can't tell you to leave, so you are welcome to stay and observe. But, do not make the mistake of thinking you are somehow in charge while you are here. That would be a grave mistake on your part."

Agent Smith looked at the sheriff for a few seconds and then nodded.

"Tell me where you're at right now and if there is anything I can do to help."

"That's more like it," said the sheriff.

He looked at Debbie and said, "Deputy, why don't you take Agent Smith to the hospital and introduce him to Jake and Randy. Maybe even let him meet Kelly in all her glory. Then run him by the Morgan and Jensen places and let him see what we've been dealing with here. And by the time you're done with that, the sun should be up and you could drive him over to Kyle's place and introduce him to Bosley and Buster. After all that, he should have a really good idea what the stakes are. I'm going to call Dean and see if I can get him down here."

"Sure thing, sheriff," she said as she stood up and grabbed her keys and weapon.

"Come with me, Agent Smith."

After she and the agent walked out the door, the sheriff just shook his head and then pulled out his cell phone and thumbed his way through his contact list.

Finding the number he was looking for, he pressed Dial.

"Hey, Dean. This is Sheriff John. Hey, we have a situation here in Prattville and I think we could use your help."

Chapter 13
~~
The hook is set

The deputy just shook her head. Standing at the door of her father's house, the last person she wanted to see, was Cindy.

"Debbie, I came as soon as I got word from Officer Jeffers."

"No, no! You shouldn't have come!"

Cindy looked at her best friend from school, for every day since, well, forever.

"When I heard that you had been injured by one of the monsters, well, I had to come."

"And you brought your son," said Debbie, as she looked down at the curly, blonde-haired boy, holding his mommy's hand. Her face dropped as she closed her eyes and begged for strength.

After a few seconds she opened her eyes and said, "Get in here, right now!"

She ushered the two of them through the door and into the living room of her father's house.

"I don't understand why you're getting so upset," said Cindy.

"Oh, do I seem upset?" asked Debbie. She could not begin to hide the frustration in her voice.

Then she leaned over and said, "Hey, Toby, why

don't you come over here and sit down."

Toby followed her to the couch and she turned on the television. She quickly rifled through the channels and found a ridiculous looking purple dinosaur dancing around and Toby's eyes lit up as he settled in to watch the show.

Debbie grabbed Cindy by the arm and hauled her into the kitchen.

"Geez, Deb. You're hurting me."

When they were out of earshot of the boy, she whirled around and hissed, "I'm hurting you! What possessed you to come over here?"

"I heard you were hurt."

"That was last week and I'm fine now!"

"Well, I'm happy to hear that. Now, what's going on?"

"You really should have called first."

"I wanted to see you. I know we don't talk like we use to, but ..."

"Cindy! It's the Boogerman!"

Cindy backed up a step, looking as if she had been slapped in the face. Debbie reached out and took her arm and helped steady her. She led her over to one of the kitchen chairs and sat her down.

As she sank down on the chair, she had a blank look on her face.

"Officer Jeffers said you had made a special trip out to see me and wanted me to call you as soon as I got back."

Debbie sat down across the corner from her friend and said, "Yes and I would have told you under no circumstances were you to come to Prattville until this is handled."

Cindy leaned forward and placed her face in her hands. She was fighting the sense that she was about to lose control and let the nightmares back in. Nightmares that she had finally been able to break free from, only just a handful of years ago.

Debbie leaned forward and touched her forehead to the top of Cindy's head.

"I was hoping we would catch this demon and send him back to Hell and we would never have to tell you about it."

Cindy sat back up and Debbie could see the absolute terror in her friend's eyes. This was exactly what she was hoping to avoid by keeping Cindy away from town.

"How many have been hurt?"

"Bill, Terry and Milly, Mike and Judy and Clara. She was the first, about two weeks ago. Randy and Jake are still in the hospital, along with Farmer Smith."

"Oh my god! This is worse than the last time."

"Yes it is, and what I need you to do," said Debbie, "is get back in your car and go home. Do not come back here until I tell you it's safe."

Cindy looked at her and said, "I'm so scared for you."

"Don't be scared for me. I've already faced him once and if I ever see his ugly mug again, my face will be the last thing he ever sees."

Cindy stood up and picked up her purse. She looked at the deputy and then reached forward and wrapped her arms around her.

"Please promise me you'll be careful."

"I promise." said Debbie as she wrapped her arms around her friend.

After a few seconds they parted and walked back into the living room. Toby was standing up in front of the couch, swaying back and forth as the purple dinosaur danced on the television screen.

"Hey, buddy, it's time to go home."

"But, mommy, you said we could have ice cream when we got here."

"We will. We'll just get it at Sophie's. You'd like to see Sophie today, wouldn't you?"

"Yes!" said the toddler, jumping up and down.

Debbie ushered them out of the house and down the path to Cindy's SUV. She got Toby settled into his car seat in the back seat and then turned to Debbie again. The worry in her eyes was very clear as Debbie reached out and squeezed her hand.

"Don't worry about me. Just get home safely. Don't stop for anything."

Cindy leaned over and kissed her on the cheek and then turned and got into her car. As they pulled away, Debbie saw Toby smiling at her through the window and she gave him a smile and a good-bye wave.

After they reached the end of the street, she pulled her phone out of her pocket and found a number and dialed.

"Tom, why in holy hell did Cindy just show up on my front doorstep?"

She waited for the answer, which was that Tom had no idea the Handleys were even back in town and would have told the chief to keep her away from Prattville at all costs.

"Well, I just sent her on her way back to Hobart. They should be getting there in less than an hour. Can you keep an eye out for her and maybe tell the chief about this, too?"

"Sure thing Debbie. By the way, how are you feeling?"

"I'm doing okay. Feeling strong and able again. We really need to put an end to this, though."

"Well, if I can be of any help let me know."

"Will do," she said as she hung up the phone.

As she stood there on the sidewalk out in front of her dad's house, it finally registered with her how dark it was. She looked up and saw all the dark, black clouds of a storm that had been rolling in all day long.

Even though it was only about six in the evening and about an hour before sunset, the dark clouds would bring total darkness much sooner than usual.

She looked down the street, in the direction of Cindy's departure and prayed that she and Toby would make it home safely. She was very close to getting her truck and going after her and escorting her all the way back to Hobart.

Then her phone rang.

"Yes, sheriff?"

After listening for a few seconds, she said, "I'll be right there."

~~~~

"What's up?" she said as she walked into the department.

Agent Smith was there and she could tell that he and her dad had already been going round and round about something.

"Agent Smith here believes we should call out the National Guard."

She looked at the fed and shook her head.

"You have got to be kidding. What in the name of all things holy would possess you to do such a stupid thing?"

The agent bristled at the inference that he didn't know how to do his job.

"You need all the help you can get on this. Too many people have died and gotten hurt and this needs to stop right now!"

"Agent Smith! If you send the National Guard into those woods, the only thing you will accomplish is giving the Boogerman more trophies for his collection."

"Oh, please. I think the US Army can handle one demon!"

"One demon that has already killed one, very large vampire, one very nasty hell hound, two goblins and a gargoyle. Do you have any clue what it took for him to have killed any of them? Your so-called US Army will be nothing more than meat puppets for him!"

Just then, a large state police officer came walking into the department and he had an orange, tiger-striped cat sitting on his shoulders.

"Good evening, Dean," said the sheriff.

The agent looked at the statie and almost laughed.

"Just what are you supposed to be? And with a cat, no less."

Dean looked at him and his eyes turned a very dark brown. The cat rose up and stood on Dean's shoulder and looked at the agent.

"Your little pussy cat don't scare me."

"Buttercup? You should be scared."

"Really? Buttercup?"

The sheriff and deputy just sat back in their chairs and watched, letting Agent Smith wrap as much rope around his neck as he wanted. John found himself wishing he had a tub of popcorn for the coming show.

There was something rattling around in the back rooms of the department and Debbie realized Mabel was probably in the back filing some paperwork.

Dean reached up and stroked Buttercup's head and then clicked his fingers. The cat jumped down off his shoulder and walked up in front of the agent and looked up at him.

Agent Smith looked down, halfway considering just kicking the cat across the room, but thought better of it.

He really didn't like cats.

But, right before his eyes, he was really glad he didn't kick the cat. He backed up and found himself with his back against a wall and the cat advancing toward him. By now the cat had grown in size and was almost up to his knees and getting bigger.

Before he had time to get himself out of there, Buttercup had grown into a very large Bengal tiger, complete with the most evil green eyes he had ever seen.

Buttercup leaned forward and brought his nose to within a couple inches of Agent Smith's nose and growled at him. The fed was pretty sure that growl had came from the pits of Hell. He turned his head and closed his eyes, quite sure he was about to have his head eaten by a freakin' tiger!

He trembled, hoping that someone would call the beast off.

In the end, his savior was an unlikely person.

He felt someone brush across the front of him and he opened his eyes slightly, just in time to see Mabel squeeze between him and under Buttercup's chin, as she came out of the back room.

As she walked past them and toward her desk, she said over her shoulder, "You two are blocking the doorway. Take it outside if you're going to fight. I don't want to have to clean up after you."

About that time John and Debbie began laughing loudly and Dean called Buttercup off.

Agent Smith stood there, up against the wall, still trembling from the horror he had just been through. He prayed that when he looked down the front of his pants would still be dry.

"We don't need no National Guard, Mr. G-man," said Debbie.

Smith walked slowly over to a chair and sat down, gripping the arms tightly to keep himself steady. He sat there for a moment, trying to gather his thoughts and catch his breath. He looked around the room and then settled on Debbie.

"You may think you don't need the National

Guard, but you need something."

Looking at Dean and Buttercup he said, "You have a mighty fine tiger there and he looks like he could handle himself in pretty much any fight he gets into. But, from what I've seen, he might not be enough. This Boogerman killed a hell hound for crying out loud. Does Buttercup stand a better chance than this Daisy did?"

Dean looked at him and said, "I'll take wagers on my friend here."

Sheriff John spoke up and said, "Look, Agent Smith, you can call out the National Guard and all that, but to do that, you'll need to go through the governor. I can assure you that you don't want to make that call."

"I don't?"

"No sir, you don't. The governor will laugh at you and he will tell you the same thing we've told you. He's not sending any regular, human troops down here just to become targets for this demon and that's all they would be."

"Have you even asked him?"

"I don't need to ask him. This isn't the first time we've had an emergency like this in town and he will not send troops down here to bail us out. We are on our own."

Smith sat back and looked at him and weighed his options.

"Okay, then tell me, what are your plans to handle this? I need to be able to tell my superiors something when I make my report this evening."

"Well, first of all, we're waiting until daylight. Then we will head back up the mountain to the demon's lair and see if we can find him there. This time, we're going in there with a full group of individuals that can handle themselves. He can take down two or three of us whenever he feels like it, but I don't think he'll be able to take a dozen of us."

Debbie snickered behind her desk, causing her dad to turn and look at her.

"Something you wanted to add, deputy?"

"You and I have both come face-to-face with the Boogerman and we're both damn lucky to come out of those encounters alive. Randy and Jake are lucky to be alive. You may find the Boogerman can't take a dozen of us attacking his lair, but I don't think it will be as easy as you think."

"I never said I thought it would be easy. I just think we'll stand a better chance with a larger group."

Debbie went to say something, but her cell phone vibrated its way across the desk and she looked at the display. She clicked her phone on and held it to her ear.

"What's up, Tom?"

After a few seconds she said, "They left here almost two hours ago, They should have gotten back an hour ago."

She listened for another few seconds and then jumped up.

"You start coming this way from there. I'm heading out."

She hung up the phone and looked at her dad and he could see the fear and worry in her eyes.

"Cindy hasn't made it back to Hobart yet."

John jumped up from his seat and grabbed his weapons belt and keys from the hook behind his desk. As they were all ready to file out of the department, they heard Mabel say, "Find her."

Debbie looked at her and nodded and then followed the others out the door.

"I'll ride with you," said John to Debbie. "Agent Smith, if you're planning on going, ride with Dean and Buttercup."

"I can ride in the back seat with you."

John looked at him and said, "If you knew how my daughter drives, you'd be thanking me for not letting you ride with us."

"Daddy!"

"Let's go," said John, as he pointed toward Dean's state police cruiser.

Agent Smith jogged around the other side of the car and climbed in as Dean was buckling up. As Smith grabbed his seat belt and pulled it over his shoulder, he felt something soft rub up against his neck. He turned to see Buttercup was sitting on the back of the seat, right behind him, rubbing his head against the side of the agent's face.

"He actually likes you." said Dean, as he slammed his car into reverse and squealed tires out onto the street. He had to race to catch up to Debbie. Or to put it more accurately, he had to race to keep her spinning lights in sight. His statie cruiser was made for patrolling the interstate highways and he still couldn't keep up with her.

"He really should think about slowing her truck down." he said under his breath.

As Smith got settled in after buckling his seat belt, Buttercup, settled down on the back of the seat with his front paws resting on the agent's left shoulder. His eyes were glued to the front windshield, staying alert for whatever they were racing toward.

The night had turned pitch black with the storm clouds overhead and the wind was up. Though there was no rain, that was probably going to change sometime soon.

Buttercup watched, knowing that something could come flying out of the dark without warning and he wanted to be ready.

Chapter 14
~~
The hunt begins

About twenty miles from Prattville, Debbie slammed on the brakes and skidded to a stop, causing Dean to do the same thing.

The sudden deceleration almost launched Buttercup through the windshield, but Agent Smith reached up and grabbed him as he flew forward and pulled him back to his lap, As the cruiser came to a stop, Buttercup stood up with his hind legs on Smith's knee and his paws on the dashboard.

A low, growl came from the cat, one that Agent Smith had already heard once before.

"Open the door and let him out or you're going to have a full grown tiger sitting in your lap."

Smith pushed the door open and the orange cat jumped out and within seconds had transformed back into a tiger. Smith and Dean bailed out of the car and walked up to the deputy's truck and found their doors open, too.

Looking forward, they saw what had caused the sudden stop.

Sitting off the road, in the high grass along the shoulder, was a late model SUV and it looked like it had been through Hell.

Debbie and the sheriff were slowly moving around the vehicle, with their guns drawn and this was the first time that Agent Smith got to see that they didn't carry conventional weapons.

Debbie moved up along the driver side of the SUV and saw the window was busted out. She felt her heart climbing in her throat as she looked in the front seat. There was some blood on the seat and on the window opening and there was some blonde hair stuck in the broken glass near the top of the door.

She was ready to cry when she heard a small whimper. Yanking the back door open, she looked in and saw Toby, still strapped into his safety seat. He had a small cut on his forehead and a little trickle of blood down the side of his face.

"Hey, buddy. How are you doing?" she said as she undid the belts holding him down.

She did a quick check of the boy, to make sure he didn't have any other injuries and when she was satisfied he was mostly unhurt, she lifted him out of the car seat. He wrapped his arms around her neck and looked at her.

"Bad man come."

"The bad man came? What did you see, Toby?" she asked as the others crowded around her.

"He smelled bad. Had fire eyes."

Debbie hugged him close, wishing she could take the image away from him.

Sheriff John asked, "Toby, did he take your mama?"

Toby didn't say anything. He just nodded slightly.

"Which way did they go?" asked Dean.

Toby turned and pointed toward the woods north of the highway. Then he looked down and saw a giant tiger.

"Kitty!" he said as he pointed at Buttercup.

The tiger moved in closer and nuzzled his nose against the outstretched hand of the toddler and Toby laughed at the touch.

Dean looked at the sheriff and said, "I think Buttercup and I are going to go for a walk."

John nodded as he turned and walked back to his cruiser. Buttercup stayed where he was, just doing what he could to keep Toby happy.

A few seconds later, they heard another siren and they could see some lights in the distance, toward Hobart.

"This isn't going to go well." said Debbie.

"Why not?" asked Agent Smith.

"That officer coming this way is from Hobart. The Chief of Police in Hobart is Chief Handley. He is Cindy's husband and Toby's father."

"Oh boy." said the agent.

As the car from Hobart pulled up, Debbie was disheartened to see that Officer Jeffers hadn't come alone.

Getting out of the passenger side was Chief Handley and he came running to the SUV.

"Oh dear God! Where is she?" he yelled.

"We don't know, chief." said the sheriff. "We just got here ourselves."

Then the chief noticed Toby in Debbie's arms.

"Toby!" he cried out.

Toby's attention was diverted from the tiger and he grinned and cried out, "Daddy!"

He reached for his daddy and Chief Handley took him from Debbie.

"Bad man took mommy."

The chief looked around and then at the sheriff.

"What does he mean *bad man*?"

"We have been battling with the Boogerman for about four weeks now and it appears that he has taken Cindy." said the sheriff.

"The Boogerman? Why the hell weren't we told he was back?" yelled the chief, scaring Toby.

Debbie stepped forward and placed a hand on Toby's arm to keep him calm.

"Chief, we didn't want to say anything because we didn't want Cindy to start having nightmares again. And we certainly didn't want her coming over here like she did today."

"She heard you had been hurt and wanted to check on you," said the chief softly.

Just then, Dean came walking back to the SUV, wearing only a bathrobe. His feet were bare and he didn't have any weapons. Agent Smith looked at him with wide eyes.

"What in the hell?"

Dean looked at the chief and nodded.

"Buttercup and I are going hunting. We're going to find your missus and bring her home."

Then he turned and looked around, then looked at Debbie.

"Avert your eyes, young lady."

"Oh please."

"Avert your eyes!"

John reached out and grabbed her by the shoulders and turned her around so her back was to the statie.

Dean took off his robe and revealed he was standing there bare ass naked. Agent Smith's eyes opened wide and John just reached out and took the robe from Dean.

Backing up a couple of steps, the statie began a transformation of his own. Within thirty seconds he became the largest, brown grizzly bear the fed had ever seen.

John released his hold on Debbie and she turned around and looked up at the bear. She reached into her pocket and pulled out a small electronic device.

"I am not a little girl. I can survive the sight of a

naked man!"

John said, "You'll always be too young for that as far as I'm concerned."

The bear looked at her and growled, blowing its hot breath in her face.

She stepped up to him and clipped the small tracking device to his fur on the underside of his neck. She started a tracking display on her smartphone and checked it and saw it was picking up the transmitter just fine.

"You two be careful out there," she said.

Dean head butted her on the shoulder and then turned and ambled off the road and toward the treeline. Buttercup fell in beside him and they disappeared into the woods.

As Smith watched them go, he said, "I'm glad I didn't take him up on that wager."

The sheriff turned around and looked at the chief.

"Take Toby and go home, chief. Debbie and I are going to follow them and we will find Cindy and bring her home."

"And me."

They turned and looked at Agent Smith.

"G-man, you have no idea what we're up against."

"I've seen the aftermath. I kind of get the idea that this is probably the most hideous, evil demon that has ever walked the Earth and I want to do whatever I can to help."

"I'll be going, too," said Tom, as he pulled his keys out of his pocket and handed them to the chief.

Looking at the chief, he said, "Get Toby out of here, sir. Protect him above all else."

The chief took the keys and nodded.

Then Tom looked at Debbie.

"You showed me what was in that truck of yours. Have an extra weapon or two that I can use?"

Debbie looked at him for a second and then half smiled and nodded her head toward the truck and started walking back.

John looked at Smith and said, "If you're going with us, you better get back there and get something for yourself. That pea shooter you have in your holster will be completely useless tonight."

The agent turned and hustled back to the truck to see what kind of weapon he could lay his hands on.

John turned back to the chief. He saw an emptiness in Handley's eyes and he knew that look well. It was the same look he had seen staring back at him from the mirror for a long time after his wife was chased off this planet.

"We'll find her. Go home."

"Please bring her home, John."

John nodded to him and the chief turned and headed back to the cruiser with his son. John just stood and watched as the chief buckled Toby into the front seat of the patrol car and then got in and left the scene.

"Don't you worry, friend," he said to himself. "He didn't kill her last time and I don't believe he'll do it this time. She's bait."

He turned around and walked to the back of Debbie's truck and looked at the other three, as they were all getting outfitted. Debbie handed a rifle looking weapon to Agent Smith and turned it on.

"You're all powered up and ready. This weapon has no safety, so be careful."

Smith looked at her and nodded that he understood.

Tom had removed his pistol from his holster and laid it in the trunk and replaced it with one monster pistol and was checking out a second pistol. He looked like he was going to be quite capable in the field.

John reached in and pulled out a rifle and turned it on. Agent Smith could feel the hair on the back of his neck stand up as the weapon's power ramped up.

Debbie had her usual assortment of weapons in her holster and hanging over her shoulders.

"Are we ready?" asked Agent Smith.

John looked at him and said, "The question is, are you ready?"

Agent Smith looked at him, with all seriousness and then raised his rifle across his chest and said,

"Absolutely."

Then accidentally fired the rifle.

The blast screamed away and slammed into a tree about a hundred yards away, causing it to split in two.

"Remember what I told you, Agent Smith?" asked Debbie. "NO SAFETY!"

"Sorry."

John looked at him like he would look at a guilty child, who had just been caught raiding the cookie jar. Then he took a deep breath and let it out.

"Okay, now that we have that out of the way, no, we're not ready just yet." he said.

"What are we waiting for?" asked Tom.

Debbie pointed down the road behind him and he could see some flashing lights coming their way. Within a few seconds, Cal pulled up and got out of his car.

"I was hoping you wouldn't leave here without me."

"We'd never cut you out of the fun, Cal." said John.

Cal pulled his rifle from the dashboard mount and walked up to the other three. He held out his hand to Tom and said, "Cal Worhl."

"Tom Jeffers, Hobart Police," he said as he shook hands with the deputy.

Agent Smith stepped forward and held out his

hand and said, "Agent Smith, Homeland Security."

Cal took his hand and said, "Yeah, I know who you are. Word gets around."

The agent took his hand back and looked like he had been slapped in the face. Cal didn't care. He had no use for the feds, probably even less than John or Debbie.

He nodded toward the burning tree and asked, "A little target practice, John?"

John grunted and shook his head.

"Don't ask."

Debbie reached out and handed two small comms devices to Tom and Smith.

"Just hook these over your ears. They are already set to our channel."

"So, what's the game plan, boss?" asked Cal.

"Dean and Buttercup took off a few minutes ago and we're going to follow their trail."

Then he looked around the group and stopped at Debbie.

"I don't suppose there's..."

"Don't you even say it." she said, shaking her head at him.

"Okay. Let's go. Let's try to stay within sight of each other."

After the three vehicles were secured, the five of them walked down off the road and through the small swale. It took a minute or so to reach the burning tree and John stopped to look at it for a second and then, shaking his head, he walked on.

It wasn't too hard for them to follow the path of the bear and tiger. They spread out a little across the path and made their way north.

For the next hour they just walked. There was no sign of anything they needed. They had started angling to the east and found themselves at the highway that went north to North Platte.

"Well, I can't say this has been very productive," said Agent Smith.

The sheriff looked at him and for a split second wondered if he would be missed in Washington if he didn't return.

"It's been a lot more productive than you think, agent."

"How so?"

"We know that's he gone back to the east side of this highway, back to his familiar territory. We also know that he took Cindy Handley on purpose. There would have been no other reason for him to be prowling the highway she was taken from."

As the agent chewed on those words, John keyed his mic.

"Hey Mabel, can you call Earl and have him bring the van and come pick us up? We're right near where Terry and Milly were attacked."

"Sure thing, sheriff."

"So, we're giving up?" asked Smith.

"What is it with you, agent?" asked Cal.

The agent looked at him and looked like he might like to go at it with Cal. Until Debbie stepped in front of him.

"No, G-man, we are not giving up. Dean and Buttercup are more than five miles in front of us and getting further away."

She showed Smith the display on her tracking device and even he could see the ping from the tracker on Dean was moving at a pretty good clip.

The sheriff looked in the direction they had been traveling.

"We're going back to our cars and moving around to the other side of town. Dean and Buttercup are on the trail of something and they are moving fast. We're going around and coming at them from the other direction."

Agent Smith nodded his understanding.

A few minutes later, Mabel pulled up with the prisoner transport van and the sheriff was not too happy about that.

"What are you doing out here, Mabel?"

"Sheriff, I am not going to cower in the department office just because this demon seems to have something against retired teachers. And watch your tone with me, young man."

"Yes, ma'am." he said as they all piled in. After

everyone was in, she turned them around and headed back to town and then back to their cars.

"Agent Smith, I need you to drive Dean's car back to the station. I am going to ride back to town with Mabel and make sure she gets back to the station house in one piece. She may think she's brave, but I don't want to have to test that."

Mabel gave him a very cool look.

He turned and looked at Tom and Cal.

"Tom, you can ride with Death Wish Debbie. After riding with her, you may reconsider any kind of relationship with her."

"Daddy!"

"I'm sure I'll survive, sheriff," Tom said with a smile.

Cal turned and headed to his truck and within seconds, they were all on their way back to town.

Debbie made a very conscious effort to maintain her speed and control of her truck with Tom sitting in the passenger seat.

She was very quiet, not saying anything for the first ten miles back to town.

"Cindy was your best friend in school, wasn't she?"

She snapped out of her thoughts and looked over at him.

"Yes, she was. She still is."

"Any idea why the Boogerman would zero in on

her?"

"I have no idea. When she was taken twenty years ago, she said he didn't try to hurt her, only kept her captive."

"And there was no indication of who this demon was?"

"No. After we found Cindy and freed her, he went on a rampage and killed five other monsters. Then he just disappeared and we never heard from him again. Not until about four weeks ago."

"Well, it sounds to me like he might have taken a liking to Cindy."

"What do you mean?"

"He didn't try to hurt her when he took her. As you say, he just kept her captive. Kind of like, he looked at her as a pet or something."

Debbie was silent for a moment and then said, "Well, he's hurt her now. All that blood and hair in her car tells me that."

"I overheard the sheriff talking to himself before. He thinks she's bait."

"That's the feeling I get, too. But bait for what?"

"You said he threatened everyone you love when he attacked you. Maybe she's bait for you. It sounds like he has something personal against you."

"When I find him, he's going to find that taking her was the single worst decision he could have made in this lifetime."

A few minutes later they crossed the bridge and drove past the Manning farm. There was a loud howl that went up and some banging coming from somewhere back on the property.

"Sounds like Buster is in full monster mode tonight," said Debbie as she looked toward the Manning house. "That is one demon dog we don't need to be chasing down tonight."

Tom thought back to the first day he had seen Debbie and how calmly and professionally she had acted that day outside of Hobart, when the demon dog was barreling toward his quiet, little town.

A couple minutes later they pulled up at the department and she could see the sheriff climbing out of the van. Cal was on his way straight through town, heading for the east side farms.

The sheriff reached up and pressed the talk button on his comms.

"I'll be back out in a second."

She nodded as he went inside with Mabel. Agent Smith parked Dean's car and then came over and said he would ride with the sheriff when he was ready to leave.

"Okay, you do that," said Debbie, "and Tom and I are going to head toward the east side of town. It looks like that's where the demon is heading."

After backing out of her parking space, she pointed the truck down the road and hit the gas. Tom felt himself pushed back into the seat as the truck launched itself into orbit.

"Take it easy, turbo."

"I thought I would show you what the sheriff is talking about. And also, I think I know where the demon is going."

"Well, you don't have to prove anything to me with your driving." said Tom as he cinched his belt a little tighter.

As they barreled through town, they were outside the town limits within one minute.

"Where do you think the demon is going?"

"I think he's heading for Farmer Taylor's place. He's already killed Clara Jensen and put Farmer Smith in the hospital. That only leaves my place and Taylor's out there."

As they screamed past her house and then by Farmer Smith's place, they could see the Taylor house had almost every light on, something Debbie knew was out of the ordinary for him. Being a vampire, he kind of liked it dark. Something must have spooked him to have him turn on all his lights.

Debbie skidded to a slow turn into the driveway and drove back. She found Cal's truck behind the house with its red and blue lights flashing and parked next to Taylor's truck.

As she turned off her engine they could hear the sounds of the fight going on somewhere north of the house. They could hear hogs screeching and could see a flash or two from Cal's rifle light up the sky.

"Sheriff, something's happening behind the Taylor place," she yelled into her comms.

"We're almost there, deputy."

Debbie and Tom bailed out of the truck and she could hear her dad's siren coming down the highway.

Tom was all for waiting for the sheriff and Agent Smith to get there, but Debbie took off running toward the sound of battle and he took off after her. Something about that made her seem more like the kind of woman he really wanted to get to know.

Chapter 15
~~
The battle for it all

Dean and Buttercup spent the better part of two hours, ambling through the dark forest, looking for any sign of the demon. If he was anywhere around, he was keeping himself well hidden.

By the time they reached the back of Farmer Taylor's land, it was just after midnight and they were thinking it was about time to turn around and head back. Dean wasn't too keen on the idea of turning back into a man after the sun came up, standing on the side of the road, naked as the day he was born.

He growled at Buttercup and the large tiger looked at him. Not quite wanting to give up just yet, he growled back, but he knew who the ultimate boss was. He turned around and they started back the way they came.

Before they had taken ten steps they heard something screeching and what sounded like an animal being slaughtered.

Both of them turned toward the sounds and then took off across the fields. It only took a few seconds for them to come out near the back of the Taylor place, but they couldn't see anything in the darkness.

They saw the lights in the farm house come on and someone charging out the back door with a shotgun.

As Dean got closer to the back fence of the hog pen, he heard another screech and saw a dark figure moving through the hogs. The hogs were all gathered together in one corner, trying to stay as far away from the creature as possible, but they were contained in a fairly strong pen, so there was no escape.

Dean could see a couple of carcasses of hogs laying in the pen, victims of the demon, but it appeared the demon was not finished.

The Boogerman lunged at the nearest hog and grabbed it and dragged it to the center of the pen and began tearing it apart. The hog squealed for a few seconds, but died mercifully as it was dismembered.

Farmer Taylor reached the pen and shouted, lowering his shotgun at the demon. The shotgun roared and the demon was knocked off its feet, skidding across the pen in the mud.

When it stood up and looked at the farmer, its red eyes blazed under its hood. Taylor wracked another round into the chamber, ready to send this demon straight back to the hell it came from, but he never got the chance.

Dean crashed through the fence, which had the happy side-effect of releasing the hogs from their captivity.

The Boogerman turned toward the rampaging

bear and tried to get away, but Dean took a massive swipe at him, knocking the demon fifty feet through the air, slamming him up against a fence post.

Buttercup was on him in the blink of an eye, growling, as he sank his fangs into the arm of the black demon.

Between the two of them they had the demon pinned to the ground and were set to do some of their own dismembering. Tearing the demon to pieces would be the highlight of their night.

Buttercup still had a good hold on the demon's arm, but he could tell that it wasn't feeling any pain. It was as if the demon's arm was only attached to its body. There didn't seem to be any pain receptors involved in the make-up of this monster.

Dean rose up, raising his front paws off the demon, getting ready to drive his paws through the monster's face. The Boogerman used that split second of freedom to drive the long nails of his freed hand into the side of the large bear and ripped away a good chunk of bear meat.

Dean felt the air get knocked out of his lungs and had to retreat a few steps. The Boogerman then used his free hand to bash the tiger upside the head, knocking it senseless for a moment.

Buttercup lost his hold on the demon's arm and as he tried to regain his senses, the monster rose up and slammed two fists into the tiger's head, knocking him out cold.

Dean saw his cat getting destroyed by the demon and that enraged him even more. Even with his injuries, he charged the Boogerman and was ready to fight to the death, but so was the monster and it was going to be the death of the bear and tiger.

As Dean closed on the demon, a dark hand with long nails swiped across the bear's midsection and opened up a large, gaping wound. Blood spilled out and Dean doubled over in pain, a pain he had never felt before when in his bear form.

Farmer Taylor yelled at the demon and when it turned, the shotgun roared to life and hit the demon square in the chest. Farmer Taylor may as well have been firing a water pistol. The blast from the shotgun did nothing, but ruffle the dark, tattered robes of the monster.

The Boogerman faced him and he could see the red eyes brighten as they glowed under the hood. As he ratcheted another round into the shotgun, the demon flew across the opening between them and drove both hands worth of long nails into the sides of the farmer.

Taylor gasped as the breath was knocked out of him and he couldn't catch his breath. The demon used his nails as hooks and pulled the farmer up and into his face. The farmer tried as hard as he could to draw a breath, but the demon was twisting his fingernails deep inside his chest, causing more pain than he had ever felt before.

The farmer could feel the lights beginning to dim in his own eyes as the demon started ripping flesh from his bones. Then he decided he needed to do something he swore he would never do again.

In a flash, the demon found himself not holding an old farmer anymore, but a very large and very angry vampire. He was even larger than Milly Oswald had been when she changed.

Taylor swiped at the demon with his own claws and shredded the hood covering the monster's head. The Boogerman retracted his nails and backed up, putting a little distance between him and the vampire.

Taylor had waited too long, though. The injuries already done to him were sufficient to weaken him to the point of not being able to fight as he could have.

The demon could feel the weakness from the vampire and started swaying back and forth.

"You should have heard your sister beg for mercy when I tore her to pieces," growled the demon.

That was the first time during this battle that Taylor had even considered that this was the demon that ended Milly's life. The thought brought renewed rage and strength and he jumped toward the demon.

His wings spread to their widest reach and there were thick, razor sharp spikes on the forward joints of the wings. As he and demon came together, he slammed one of the spikes into the side of the Boogerman's head and there was an audible crunch, but it was completely ineffective.

The demon just backed away a few steps and shook it off. As the sheriff had suspected, this demon had to be walking between the living world and the dead world. And right now, he was mostly in the dead world, beyond the reach of the spikes, claws and guns of the living world.

The Boogerman closed the gap again and drove his right hand up and under the chin of the vampire, extending his nails and driving them right through and out the top of Taylor's head.

In an instant, Taylor saw the lights flicker in his mind and then they went out completely. He slumped to his knees, his body being held upright by the demon.

The Boogerman slowly extended one nail from one of his fingers on his left hand and in a swift motion, slashed across the neck of the vampire, separating his head from his body.

He let the body of the defeated vampire drop to the ground, falling into a growing pool of its own blood. He lifted the head up and stared into its lifeless eyes.

A low rumbling laugh could be heard coming from the demon's belly and he lifted the head up high and screeched.

Then he heard a groaning coming from behind him and turned to see that Dean had returned to human form and was holding his sides where the demon had slashed him.

"Aww, you should have stayed as a bear." said the Boogerman. "I don't want any human heads in my collection."

He stood over the statie and dripped vampire blood all over him, laughing as he did it.

"Well, I guess I do want a few human heads. The sheriff's, the deputy's and that stupid bitch, Cindy."

"You leave them alone!" coughed Dean as he tried to shield himself from the blood the demon was sprinkling on him.

"Or what? What are you going to do about it?"

"Hey, jackass!"

The Boogerman whirled around to see Cal vaulting over the hog pen fence, bringing his rifle to bear. A split second later it erupted and the ball of light hit the demon square in the midsection, knocking him backwards and out of the hog pen. The vampire head went flying through the air, landing near the unconscious Buttercup.

Cal pointed again and fired as he ran up next to Dean. This time, the ball of light just passed right through the demon and exploded on a tree behind him.

Cal fired again and got the same result.

"He's phased into the dead world," gasped Dean.

"Shit!" said Cal as the demon started toward him.

Cal dropped the rifle into Dean's outstretched hand and pulled his knife. He flipped a switch on the handle and the blade started glowing along the outside edge. He braced himself for the impact of the demon.

He switched the knife to his right hand and stepped into the oncoming demon and drove the blade as deep as he could into the monster's chest. The Boogerman acted like he didn't even feel it and caught Cal upside the head with a roundhouse punch. The deputy flew across the hog pen and slammed up against one of the posts, knocking the breath out of him.

As he struggled to get back on his feet, he could see the demon closing on him and he tried to shake off the cobwebs before the attack reached him.

Then a streak of orange and black flashed across his field of vision and Buttercup took the demon to the ground, but only for a second. Buttercup was a shifter, but he was still very much in this world and had little effect on the Boogerman.

As they rolled across the ground, the tiger came to his feet and turned to face the demon and let out a roar that split the night. He started prowling closer to the demon, who was just standing still, swaying back and forth. Buttercup was looking for that one split second when he could charge and get his teeth into the demon and rip him to pieces.

He didn't have to wait long because the Boogerman decided to bring the fight to him. The demon charged and so did Buttercup, but the demon was far stronger than anyone thought he should be. He pounded a fist against the side of the charging tiger's head and knocked him easily to the side.

Buttercup staggered, but wasn't ready to admit defeat and turned back to the fight. He was just about ready to charge again when a flash happened and the demon caught another ball of energy in the midsection. This one was enough to knock him across the hog pen.

Cal looked up to see Debbie coming through the gate and fire round after round into the demon. He also saw Tom firing like his life depended on it, most likely believing that it did. Cal struggled to his feet and called Buttercup away from the demon.

The tiger was reluctant to walk away from the fight, but he also didn't like being around those rifles when they were being fired. They caused his fur to stand on end and he didn't like that.

The demon charged Debbie, as if he had his sights set on her specifically, as if she was his real target. Just before he got to her, Tom jumped in between the two of them and fired again and again. All he got for his troubles was Debbie yelling at him to get out of the way and a heavy, pounding swing of the demon's right hand that caught him in the ribs. He flew through the air and landed at Cal's feet. Buttercup looked down at him and put a paw on his back to keep him down.

Debbie pulled a pistol from her holster and flipped a switch and started firing. This time the blasts from the gun had an effect and caused the demon to back away and screech in pain. She kept firing, one shot after another, driving the demon backward.

But, no matter how advanced their weapons were, the batteries could only power them for a limited amount of time and Debbie's pistol decided to give up the ghost at the worst possible moment.

When her trigger clicked silently, the demon bullrushed her, knocking her to the ground. She tried to fire again, but it was no use. That pistol was down for the count until she had time to recharge it and she doubted the Boogerman would give her a timeout so she could do that.

As the Boogerman stood over her, He reached down and smashed his fist against her face, knocking her out completely. Cal fired again, but he knew his weapon would have no effect on the monster. He just wanted to distract him. The demon stopped what he was doing and looked at Cal. His red eyes flashed brighter and he turned to face the tall deputy, thinking it would be nice to add his head to the collection.

He started toward Cal and Buttercup lowered his body, getting ready to pounce, but they never got the chance. The Boogerman was knocked off his feet by another blast. He came up screeching in frustration because he just couldn't finish what he had set out to do. He whirled around and caught another blast in the gut.

This time the charge passed through him and he saw Sheriff John advancing toward him, pulling his own pistol from his holster. The demon knew that there was something special about these pistols and he was feeling their effect and when the sheriff fired, the blast knocked him fifty feet backward, cartwheeling across the ground.

His momentum didn't stop at all. He came up and continued his flight and vanished into the trees, wanting to get away from this battle that was causing him more pain that he wanted to deal with.

Agent Smith started firing his rifle into the trees and went running after the demon, but he was called off by the sheriff.

"We have to stop him!" yelled the fed.

"And we will, Agent Smith. But, if you go chasing after him by yourself, with that rifle, he'll have no problem adding your head to his collection."

Buttercup let Tom up off the ground and he ran to

Debbie, finding her completely unconscious and sporting a nice bruise on the side of her face. He reached out and brushed her hair off her face and she started to rouse. She looked up at him through some very blurry eyes and smiled.

"Good morning."

Tom laughed and ran his hand over her cheek, which brought a little yelp of pain from her.

"Does that remind you where you are?" asked Tom.

She closed her eyes and shook her head. Then she opened her eyes and looked around.

"Where is he?"

"He ran away like the pussy he is when your dad showed up."

She sat up and looked around, seeing her dad a little ways off. She saw Cal and Agent Smith talking with each other.

"Where is Buttercup?" she asked.

"He took off into the woods after the Boogerman a few minutes ago. Those other two are getting ready to follow after him and I'm going with them. You stay here and rest."

She looked up at him and he could see the fire in her eyes.

"Look, Debbie, he's been pounding on you ever since he came back." said Tom. "I think it's time for you to sit back for a few minutes and let someone else get pounded on."

She looked at him and then asked, "How are you feeling? I know he clubbed you pretty good."

"I've probably got a couple of cracked ribs, but nothing serious."

He looked up and saw Cal and Agent Smith getting ready to head into the woods. He looked back down at her.

"You be careful, Tom" she said.

"I promise I will if you stay here."

She gave him a pouty look, but she knew she was in no shape to stand up right then anyway.

"Alright."

Tom leaned over and kissed her on the forehead.

"Eww. Another kiss from you and we haven't even had a second date."

"We'll get to that." he laughed as he stood up and started after the other two.

She rolled her head to the side and watched him go, waiting for him to disappear into the trees.

"Don't tell me to stand down." she said under her breath.

Chapter 16
~~
In the clutches of the demon

Debbie rolled over and onto her knees and then she pushed herself up off the ground. As she looked around the field, the devastation was heartbreaking. Everywhere she looked, she saw dead and dying.

Farmer Taylor was dead, having been torn to pieces by the demon. Oh, and losing his head. That tends to have a detrimental effect on a person's health.

About half his hogs were also dead. Those that weren't dead, soon would be.

She looked back toward the tree line and saw her dad trying to give aid to Dean. She staggered across the open field to the sheriff and by the time she reached him, she had shaken off the cobwebs and mist in her head.

She found her dad working on stopping the bleeding in the statie's side. He had changed back into a human and he laid on the ground, clenching his side where the demon had ripped out a huge chunk of flesh.

"You should have stayed in bear form, Dean. You'd be stronger." she said.

As she knelt down next to Dean, her father looked at her and asked, "Are you alright?"

"Yes, sheriff. Just a little bruised, but I'm fine."

Dean looked up at her and said, "I'll be fine, sweetie. Your dad's done a good job of patching me up."

She looked toward the treeline where the other three had gone.

"I'm going after them." she said to her dad.

"Damn it, Debbie! You'll do no such thing."

"Daddy! Stop trying to protect me! He's attacked me twice now and I still live. I think he's just playing with us."

"I think he wants to draw you out."

"Well, it's working and he's going to wish it hadn't."

She checked her weapons and then said, "Give me your spare GZ-7 battery. Mine's dead."

Her dad looked up at her and said, "Suppose I said I don't have one?"

"I'd know you were lying. You always have a couple of spares."

As he reached into his inside jacket pocket, he asked, "Which begs the question, why don't you have a spare or two?"

"Bailed out of the truck too fast and didn't have time to grab a couple."

He pulled a spare battery from his pocket and

handed it to her.

"I should make you walk back to your truck and get them."

She snatched the battery from his hand and slammed it into the pistol, bringing a welcome hum as it powered up.

"I promise to start carrying them on my person from this day forward, sheriff."

Then she looked down at Dean and he looked up at her and nodded slightly.

"You be careful, little girl," he wheezed.

"I'm going to find Buttercup. Once I do, I'll have a Grade-A battle companion."

She looked at her dad and then turned to head for the trees. Her dad called after her.

"You keep your comms on, deputy. And that's an order!"

"Absolutely."

She headed into the trees and started following the trail that was laid out through the woods. She knew these woods pretty well, within a mile or so of the back of her property. She walked in the woods all the time. But, if she got more than a couple of miles into the back woods, she was out of her element.

She followed the trail until the point it became less familiar to her. She kept her rifle pointing straight ahead, with the flashlight turned on. She kept the light swinging back and forth across the path, looking for a large, orange and black tiger. Buttercup had to be out there somewhere, but she didn't know where.

She could feel the hum of the pistol in the holster on her hip and it brought a measure of calm to her nerves.

After about a half hour, her dad called to say that Dean had been picked up by the paramedics and he was coming into the woods behind her. He asked her to stop and wait for him, but he knew that was a lost cause. Debbie told him where she was and where she was going and he could catch up to her.

They had a really hard time understanding each other because there was a lot of static on the channel.

John followed the trail as best as he could, but after about a half hour, he knew he had lost his way and was not anywhere near finding her. He called to her on the comms, but didn't get an answer. He called again and got nothing, but static. He pulled the earpiece off and checked it to see it was registering a full charge, but there was a crack in the plastic shell. It must have happened during the encounter with the Boogerman and he knew it was dead to the world now. He clicked the power button off and stuffed it into his pocket.

He stopped and listened to the night around him. There were the usual sounds of the night critters in the air and also the sound of a large, demon dog howling at the full moon.

"You just stay in your pen, Buster," he muttered under his breath.

~~~~

Cal, Tom and Smith were about halfway back to the north bound highway and they all knew they were in the middle of a dangerous situation. It was just the three of them and they had no hope of any backup nearby.

"Shouldn't we be thinking of heading back?" asked Smith.

"Getting a little scared, are you, agent?"

Smith looked at the back of the deputy and came to a stop where he was. Cal turned and looked at him. Tom stepped forward, just in case there was any violence. He knew that Cal had no respect for the fed and didn't have any trouble showing it.

"Yes, deputy, I am getting a little scared and if you had half a brain in your head you'd be getting scared, too. Or are you some monster that hasn't been revealed to me yet?"

The deputy stepped right in front of the agent.

"Agent Smith, I am terrified right now. We're out here by ourselves and who knows what else is around here. But, we have a job to do."

They stood there looking at each other for a few seconds.

"You didn't answer my other question." said Smith.

Cal half smiled and then said, "No, Agent Smith. I am not a monster of any kind. Born and raised on the family farm in southern Iowa and the worst monster I'd ever seen before coming here was the evil, Angus bull we had on the farm."

Smith nodded at him and then said, "Martin."

"Excuse me?"

"My name is Martin. I know you and the others are kind of laughing about my name being Smith, which it really is. But, call me Martin."

Cal looked at him and then held out his hand.

"Good to have you here with us, Martin."

Tom breathed a sigh of relief. The last thing he wanted to do was go toe-to-toe with the big deputy.

~~~~

Debbie continued north on the path she was on. The path was becoming more difficult to navigate the further she went. The brush was growing across the path and she was making a lot more noise than she really wanted to. She didn't like advertising her approach to anyone or anything.

After about twenty more minutes, she came over a small rise in the path and stopped. There was something on the far side of a small clearing the path bisected, but it was hidden in the shadows of the trees on the other side.

She dropped down to her knees and then to her belly. All her training from the military came back and she started low crawling forward, moving just a couple of inches at a time, trying to be as quiet as she could.

She reached the edge of the clearing and had some tall grass to hide her if anyone looked her way. She still couldn't make out what was going on over on the other side of the clearing. She was only about twenty yards away, but whatever it was, it was too dark to see it clearly.

The hairs standing up on the back of her neck told her exactly what she was looking at though. She could hear the demon and it sounded like he was eating something.

Then her heart just about jumped out of her throat when something brushed up against her cheek. She jerked away from it and found herself looking into the green eyes of an orange and white tabby cat.

"Damn it, Buttercup!" she hissed as quietly as she could.

The cat just leaned forward and rubbed the top of his head against the back of her hand. And he purred. He purred so loud Debbie was quite sure the Boogerman would be able to hear it.

"Stop that!" she said as quietly as she could.

Then she pointed across the clearing and Buttercup rose up a little to take a look. Then he sank back down and growled very quietly. Then proceeded to change back into a Bengal tiger. Debbie was amazed at how quietly he did that.

Buttercup didn't take his eyes off the target, but growled very softly. If she hadn't been laying right next to him, she knew she never would have heard it. She turned her eyes back to the front and looked.

As their sight became a little more accustomed to the dim light of the moon, they could see the Boogerman was just outside the edge of the moonlight and was eating one of the hogs that he had dragged away from the farm. He had his back toward her and Buttercup and was hunched over, enjoying his meal.

Debbie set her rifle down and pulled the pistol from her holster. She sighted down the barrel and if the demon had been facing her, it would have seen the glow of her weapon, but with his back to her, he didn't see anything.

As she prepared to fire, she could feel Buttercup beginning to tense up, getting ready to pounce when the gun fired. He was going to be on this demon within a second when the time came and he wanted to rip him apart for what he did to Dean.

Debbie began to tighten her finger on the trigger and was within a split second of firing the weapon, when the trigger emitted a small, barely audible click. But, it might as well have been a stick of dynamite. The click was a foreign sound to the nighttime on the mountainside and the Boogerman whirled around when he heard it.

Debbie fired, but the shot went wide when the demon moved one way and then the other. He came charging across the clearing, but was waylaid by an attacking tiger. The tiger charged him and knocked him down, scraping the demon's body along the ground.

He went to sink his fangs into the demon and try to rip its heart out, but the Boogerman was still a strong, formidable force and he clubbed the tiger upside the head with one bony hand, knocking Buttercup off of him and across the clearing.

Debbie jumped to her feet and fired again, again missing when the demon rolled away from the tiger. She took a couple of steps closer, trying to get so close she couldn't miss, but the demon was about as fast as any monster she had ever seen.

Buttercup attacked again and drove the demon to the ground and Debbie ran up, jamming her pistol into the side of the Boogerman. She pulled the trigger and felt the blast as it hit the demon in the side, but the blast also scared the tiger and he jumped back, allowing the demon back to its feet.

Debbie couldn't believe the demon was still

upright and mobile after she had just shot him point blank. She saw that she needed to avoid using the weapon around Buttercup, not wanting to startle him again.

The demon charged her and Buttercup lunged and grabbed him by the arm. The Boogerman screeched in pain as the tiger bit down hard. The tiger wrenched the demon's arm back and forth, dragging him around like a broom on a floor.

As the attack was going on, the hood of the demon fell off its head and Debbie finally got a good look at the demon's face. Even though it was dark, the moonlight was bright enough in the clearing for her to see it.

His face was as black as night, with those two red eyes buried back in the sockets of his skull. He had skin stretched across his skull, that looked like black leather that was two sizes too small.

Buttercup drove him to the ground again and dropped his full weight on the demon.

Debbie brought the pistol right up to the face of the demon. Buttercup stopped trying to kill the demon right there, but still held him down. The demon looked at the weapon pointed at its face and Debbie could have sworn it was laughing.

"You can't hurt me with those pathetic weapons." growled the demon.

Buttercup reached up with one massive paw and

pressed it against the demon's head and held him down.

"No, maybe I can't." said Debbie. "But I wouldn't test the tiger if I were you. He's ready to tear your head off."

The Boogerman looked up and into the eyes of the tiger. His blazing, green eyes were glowing with anger.

"He wants so bad to end you right here, right now," said Debbie.

"Do it!" screeched the demon. "Do it and you will never see your pretty, little friend again!"

Debbie pressed the end of the pistol barrel into the cheek of the demon and Buttercup removed his paw from the demon's head and placed it in the middle of his chest, along with his other front paw. Raising up he put as much weight as he could on the chest of the demon, causing the demon to struggle for breath.

"Where is she?" yelled Debbie.

"Oh, she's somewhere safe. For now."

Debbie pressed the pistol into the cheek of the demon even harder.

"Where is she? I won't ask again."

"Good, because I tire of hearing your insipid voice," growled the demon.

Debbie knew she was at a standstill with the demon right now. She could threaten to kill him all night long and the demon acted like he didn't care one bit. She backed away from the demon and Buttercup looked up at her, wondering what she wanted him to do.

This gave the demon just a split second to get one of his hands on a large rock and bash it against the tiger's head. Buttercup went down like a sack of rocks.

In a flash, the demon was up and on Debbie before she had time to react. Out of the corner of her eye she saw the demon swing and his balled up fist caught her on the side of the head. The other side of the face from where she had been hit earlier. She knew she was going to have some very colorful bruises by the time this night was over.

She felt the shock of the blow and there was a flash of light, which she was quite sure was her brain getting smashed against the inside of her skull.

Then the lights went out.

In the distance, she could hear howling.

~~~~

It took John quite a long time to find the clearing. He could hear Debbie's weapon discharging, but he had gone the wrong way, so it took him a few minutes to get back. When he got there, he found an unconscious tiger on the ground. He also found

Debbie's rifle and pistol laying on the ground. One other thing he found, brought his heart into his throat. Laying in the grass, he saw a blinking light and when he picked it up, he was staring at her comms unit.

"Debbie!"

Nothing, but silence greeted his ears.

Chapter 17

~~

It all makes sense now

Debbie slowly began to rouse from her unconsciousness, trying to shake off the effects of the beating she took. It took a couple of minutes for her to realize she was no longer in the clearing, no longer near Buttercup and no longer in possession of her weapons.

Another thing that became very clear was her hands were tied behind her back and around a post. After she opened her eyes, she looked around and saw she was in a barn and tied to one of the support posts in the middle of the barn. It really gave her the creepy crawlies to think she had been carried by the Boogerman to this barn and tied up. She wondered just what the demon had in mind for her.

She scanned the inside of the barn and didn't see the demon anywhere, but she did see something else that almost brought her to tears.

Cindy was tied up to a post about five feet away and she looked like she was unconscious, too. There was blood on her face and down the front of her blouse. Debbie could see that she was breathing, but that was the only movement she saw from her friend.

She reached out with one of her feet and nudged

Cindy's foot, bringing a small moan from the captive mother. She kicked her foot again and Cindy's eyes flew open in terror. When she saw Debbie looking back at her, she couldn't decide if she was dreaming or if this was real.

"Debbie?"

"Hey girlfriend. How are you feeling?"

Cindy looked at her and said, "Not too good. How long have I been here?"

"Just a few hours. We found your truck and started searching immediately."

"Oh my God! Toby!"

"He's okay, sweetie. He's with your husband."

Cindy let out a breath of relief.

"Why is this happening to us?' she cried, looking at Debbie. She hoped there was some sort of grand plan to get them out of this, to save their lives.

"I don't know. It appears this demon has been holding a grudge for over twenty years, back to the first time you were taken. The people he's been killing have all been teachers at one time or another."

"So, you think this goes back to when we were kids?"

"It looks that way."

Debbie looked around and studied the interior of the barn. It was pretty dark and she couldn't see a whole lot, but she began to realize she had been there before.

"This isn't the same barn we found you in twenty years ago?"

"No, I don't think it is. As a matter of fact, I'm pretty sure of it. I used to see that barn in my nightmares almost every night. This isn't the same one."

Debbie felt sorry for her friend, knowing that those nightmares which she had just recently been free of, were about to come crashing back into her mind. The rest of her life was going to be filled with tormented dreams of this new horror.

"I just hope my dad and the others can find this place in time. They are on the way, just so you know."

She was about to say something else when there was a crash at the door and it flew open. The Boogerman came floating into the barn. This was the first time she realized that the demon didn't actually walk on the ground, but floated a few inches above it. Maybe Dean was right when he said this creature existed in both the living and dead planes.

"Back to get your ass kicked?" spit Debbie.

The demon looked at her and started laughing. His laugh came from deep down inside his evil body and his tattered, black robe shook all over when he did it.

"Keep laughing numb nuts. Untie me and I'll really give you something to laugh at."

The demon dropped down until he was face-to-face with Debbie, his wretched breath causing her to want to spew in his face.

"Ewww, when was the last time you brushed your teeth?"

"You should be a little more careful about what you say."

"Why? You don't scare me. And why put the hood back up? I've already seen your Halloween mask."

The demon continued to stare at her, his burning red eyes glowing from underneath his hood. Then, he reached up and pushed the hood back off his head, revealing the hideous face Debbie had seen earlier. He was missing about half his teeth and those he still had were a mixture of yellow and black. He had the breath to match. His nose was large and flat, looking like it had been broken many times in the past.

"Oooo, a face only a mother could love." said Debbie.

As she looked closer, she saw the spot where she had driven her thumb through his cheek and could see that the wound was still there.

"Oh, I hope that hurt," she said, looking at the hole in his cheek.

"I don't feel much pain anymore."

"Oh really? And why is that?"

"Being a demon that is neither alive or dead finds that pain is a distant memory."

She could feel the hot breath of the demon on her

face.

"How about the piece of meat you lost to Milly? From your ribs, right?"

"That old lady didn't stand a chance," laughed the demon.

"And yet, she took a piece of your hide during that little fight. When I get loose, I'm going to take a lot more."

The Boogerman looked at her and then smiled with his rotten mouth.

"You should really learn a little respect."

"For you? You're kidding, right?"

"For what I can do."

"I already told you, you don't scare me."

"Maybe I don't scare you, but I'll bet I scare your little friend here."

He glided backwards until he was even with Cindy. He reached out and stroked her cheek with one of his long fingernails. Cindy tried to turn away from him, but he grabbed her by the cheeks and turned her face back toward his. He leaned in and brought his decaying lips to hers and planted a disgusting kiss on her mouth. Cindy tried to pull away, but she couldn't go anywhere.

"Leave her alone!" yelled Debbie.

"Or what?" laughed the demon.

"Like I said, untie me and we'll find out."

The Boogerman moved around until he was

behind Cindy, who looked like she wanted to throw up. She was never going to be able to get the taste of that demon out of her mouth.

The demon ran a long fingernail up the side of her cheek, stroking her pale, soft skin. She closed her eyes and her whole body shuddered at the touch of this filth. Debbie could imagine the horror that was flowing through Cindy's mind and wanted so bad to rescue her from it.

"Is this the only way you can get girls?" Debbie asked the demon, trying to draw his attention away from Cindy.

"What the hell do you know?" spat the demon as he drifted quickly back across the gap to her.

"That's it, isn't it? You can't get the girls unless you kidnap them and tie them up in a barn. If you don't do that, they just ignore you."

"Shut up!" roared the demon.

"I knew it! You're a damn loser when it comes to the babes."

Cindy kept watching and listening, wondering just how much more the demon would take from Debbie before he decided to kill her. She halfway wished her friend would stop. This demon was capable of killing just for the sheer pleasure of it.

However, at the same time, she wished she could be as brave as Debbie in the face of this horror. She admired her friend who would sooner spit in the face of the demon than show any fear.

"I said shut up!" screamed the demon, his spittle flying into Debbie's face.

"Ewww. Say it, don't spray it, man," said Debbie.

The demon leaned in, his lips just an inch or so from her lips.

"Maybe I'm wasting my affections on the wrong woman."

"Not really. You're not exactly my type. I prefer humans."

He leaned in even closer and she turned her head away. Then got completely grossed out when he licked the side of her face with his black tongue.

"Oh gross! I'm going to have to take about ten showers to wash that off."

"I've always wondered what you would taste like, Deputy Dinkie."

She turned her face to him and he could see the fire in her eyes.

"Oh, that's right. You don't like to be called that."

She recoiled and then spit in his face. He just laughed and wiped his face and then became even more repugnant to her by licking his fingers.

Then she looked even closer at him. He was talking as if he knew her and Cindy from their childhood.

"Who are you?"

"I'm the Boogerman. Don't you recognize me?"

"No, I mean, who are you when you're not the Boogerman."

"Oh, you haven't figured that out yet. Such a shame."

"How could I? I don't remember anyone from years ago as ugly as you."

She could feel the anger building in him. She could see it in his eyes and she knew she was starting to get to him.

If she was going to die, she was going to do so by pissing him off more than anyone ever had. It became her personal quest. Besides, if she could get him enraged enough, he might make a mistake and give her and Cindy a chance.

In the distance, she could hear that howling again. The full moon was high in the sky and she knew Buster was in full demon dog mode. She only hoped he was being nice to Bosley. She felt sorry for the hell hound.

The Boogerman rose up and started moving back and forth in front of her. If his feet were touching the ground, she would have said he was pacing. One thing she could see was the frustration he was letting take hold in his mind. If he had a mind.

She glanced at Cindy and was surprised to see her friend trying to hide a grin. There was a twinkle in her eye that Debbie remembered from many years ago.

She smiled back at her, trying to let her know that they weren't going to die. At least, not tonight.

The Boogerman caught her looking at Cindy and smiling and dropped down right in her face.

"You think this is funny?" he growled.

"I think you are."

The Boogerman reached back and then slapped her hard across the face. Try as hard as she could, she couldn't stifle the yelp of pain that escaped from her mouth when his hand struck.

She could taste the blood in her mouth as she looked back at him with every ounce of anger she could muster.

"You will not live to see the sun rise, demon," she growled through clenched teeth.

"No," he said as he rose back up, "it's you that won't live much longer. But, to give you the answer to the question that seems to be burning in the front of both of your minds, let me show you."

Then they both watched as the Boogerman began to change. He was getting smaller and began dropping to the ground, when his feet became more human in appearance.

Debbie pulled both of her feet up, bending her knees in front of her. She didn't want to come in contact with whatever this demon was becoming.

It took almost a full minute and when the change was complete, there was a grown man, about thirty years old, standing between the two of them.

Debbie looked up and she couldn't believe her eyes. It was like something out of a bad dream.

"Kenny Kline? Are shitting me?" she gasped.

He looked down at her and grinned.

"You never would have guessed it was me."

"No, not in a million years. What the hell, Kenny?"

"Have you forgotten the way you treated me back when we were kids?"

"You were a schoolyard bully! Nobody liked you!"

"Well, I liked Cindy, but because she was your friend, you kept her away from me!"

"Oh, so you kidnapped her thinking that was the way to win her heart?"

"I just wanted her to see me for who I truly was."

"Oh, believe me, she sees it right now."

Kenny turned and looked at Cindy, who was just shaking her head.

"All this because you had a schoolboy crush on me. I can't believe it."

"I liked you, Cindy. I wanted you to like me back."

"You were a mean, cruel boy in school. What ever made you think I would like a boy like you?"

Kenny looked at her and the two of them could see he was starting to shake with anger.

He turned back to Debbie and screeched.

"See what you did! You turned her against me!"

"Why are you targeting all the teachers?" asked Debbie.

"Ever since that day you hit me, they started watching me a lot closer. My life in school became a living hell!"

"A living hell? What do you call what you put all the other kids through? And you killed those five teachers back then."

Kenny shifted back and forth on his feet, trying to control his anger. He had a vague idea that she was trying to get him pissed off, but he really didn't care.

Neither one of these women was going to walk out of that barn alive.

"Just untie us, right now," said Debbie as calmly as she could.

"Oh no," he bellowed as he took a couple steps toward her. "I intend to make good on my promise and kill both of you and everyone you both love."

This was the moment Debbie was waiting for. As he got closer to her, her left foot shot out and connected with his kneecap and the sound of his knee snapping bounced off the walls of the barn. As he was falling forward, she kicked as hard as she ever had with her right foot and her heavy boot caught him right under the chin, dropping him like a sack of rocks. He was out cold before his nose hit the floor, probably breaking it again.

"Great," said Cindy. "But, we're still tied up."

"Not for much longer, sweetie." said Debbie.

She closed her eyes and began to center herself, preparing to draw on the strength she had known since her birth. When she was ready, she began to pull her wrists apart as hard as she could and she could feel the rope beginning to separate behind her.

As she was just about to break the rope, Kenny started to stir and she knew she didn't have much more than a few seconds. With one last surge of effort, the rope snapped and her arms came free and around in front of her.

She immediately crabbed the few feet to Kenny, who was just beginning to push himself up, and she rolled him onto his back and jumped on his chest.

All the emotions and anger that she felt when she was just eight years old, came flooding back and she began to wail on his face, making sure to break his nose again in the process.

"You are nothing, but a dog turd, you piece of crap!" she yelled as she hit him over and over.

"Debbie!"

It took a second for the sound of her name to register and she stopped and looked at Cindy.

"He's out again. You can stop."

She looked down at the bloody, mangled face of Kenny and for a second, she saw the eight year old boy she had beaten up in the third grade. He was still breathing, but it was a ragged, raspy breath.

She climbed off him and grabbed the rope she had broken. She flipped the demon man over and tied his hands behind his back and then hog tied him just for extra measure.

Then she dropped down behind Cindy and untied her hands and helped her up. As they got to their feet, Cindy threw her arms around Debbie's neck and started crying. Debbie wrapped her arms around her friend and just held her tight. She could feel her sobs as she fought to regain control of her emotions.

"It's okay, sweetie. It's over."

As they stood there, holding each other tight, relieved that it was over, they forgot to keep an eye on Kenny. In his human form, the ropes were more than enough to hold him. They just didn't notice that he was changing back into the Boogerman and the ropes weren't going to be nearly enough to contain him.

It was Cindy that noticed the dark figure rising up behind Debbie and when she screamed, the deputy knew exactly what was happening.

She spun around and caught a demon fist on the side of her face, but it was a glancing blow and wasn't enough to knock her out, though it did knock her across the barn and up against a pile of scrap lumber.

She heard Cindy begging for Kenny to stop, even

promising to be his friend. All he had to do was stop. The Boogerman started floating toward Cindy, with his arms stretched out and Debbie knew there was no stopping him this time.

She climbed to her feet and picked up a discarded ax handle at the same time and took a couple of steps across the barn. Kenny was so intent on killing Cindy right then and there, he didn't see the ax handle coming around at his head. When it connected, he was knocked right out of the air and slammed into a post, shaking the entire barn with the impact.

Debbie reached forward and grabbed Cindy by the wrist and dragged her toward the door. In two steps she raised her right foot and kicked the door right off its hinges and opening their way to freedom.

As they ran out of the barn, Debbie pushed Cindy toward the path leading away and down the mountain.

"Run! Get away from here!"

Cindy stopped and looked at her.

"What are you doing? You can't stay here!"

"I can and I will. This is going to end right here and now. Now go!"

She turned Cindy back to the path and pushed her toward it. The young mother started running as fast as she could. She was never the athletic type, but when your life is on the line, it's amazing how much you can do.

Cindy hated herself for running and leaving her friend to deal with the monster that had terrorized her for so many years. The only reason that it became acceptable to her was the image that flashed through her mind of Toby and her husband. She needed to live, if for no other reason than seeing them again.

She could hear the same howling she had been hearing most of the night, but somehow it sounded a lot closer. It was definitely two different animals making that sound. She wasn't quite sure she wanted to find out what was actually raising all that noise and hoped she wouldn't run into it.

After a couple of minutes, she could hear the battle had started behind her. There was the familiar screech of the Boogerman and she could even hear Debbie yelling at him, that she was going to take him apart, piece by piece. That only brought another roar of rage from the demon and more crashing.

She stopped and dropped to her knees right there in the middle of the path. She cried even harder, knowing that Debbie was back there, fighting the Boogerman all by herself.

Never having been a very religious person, she was surprised to find herself bowing her head and closing her eyes. She was asking for anyone out there listening, to help save her friend from the attack. Though she didn't necessarily believe in God, she felt there was something out there in the universe that was much stronger than her and that's who she called out to.

The answer to her prayers came in a very unexpected form. Actually, in two unexpected forms. As she knelt there in the middle of the path, she was shocked to feel a very wet, very sloppy nose rub up against her cheek.

She slowly opened her eyes and found herself staring into the burning, red eyes of a hell hound. She fell backward on her butt and just stared at the monster dog.

Woof.

She could tell by that one sound from the hell hound, that he meant her no harm. But, she wasn't quite so sure about the very large, black mass that was standing right behind him.

Then she remembered the story her husband had told her a month ago, about a large, black dog that had tried to come to Hobart and how Debbie had stopped it.

She scrambled to her feet and found herself looking at Bosley and Buster and they just looked at her. She wasn't sure what to do, when there was another sound of battle coming from behind her. She looked and then turned back to the two demon dogs and pointed back up the path.

"Save Debbie!"

She had to jump out of the way as the two

monster dogs raced past her and toward the sound of the fight. Then she turned and ran back up the path, following them, looking to help her friend in any way she could.

Chapter 18
~~
The final battle

Debbie shifted the ax handle back and forth in her hands, staying in a defensive crouch, ready for anything the demon might try.

"Do you really think you have what it takes to defeat me?" raged the Boogerman.

"Oh please," she said. "You're nothing more than an adolescent, little boy that didn't get the present you wanted for Christmas and now you're throwing a temper tantrum."

The Boogerman charged her again and was able to swipe at her with one of his hands, raking her shoulder with his long fingernails, but it wasn't enough to take her down.

She brought the ax handle up and under the chin of the demon, driving him backward and away from her.

"You're not completely human, are you?' growled the demon.

"Whatever gave you that idea?" said Debbie as they circled each other again.

"Because you fight like you got some monster blood in you."

"Whatever it takes to remove your heart and stuff

it down your throat!"

The demon advanced again and she drove the end of the ax handle right between those red eyes, knocking him backward. She knew she needed to keep up the attack, so she advanced, hitting him again in the face and then in the chest. Each time she struck, he fell back another two or three steps.

Then she made the mistake of trying to go for the kill and swinging the handle, she was going to drive his head right out of the park. But, he ducked and she missed, throwing her off balance.

He brought one of his hands up and drove his fingernails right into her side, driving the breath from her lungs. She felt like she had just been shot in the ribs with a shotgun.

There was a gasp of pain that escaped from her lips and she could almost feel the glee the demon was experiencing right then. She couldn't draw another breath to be able to cry out in pain and felt the fog of agony wash over her as the demon twisted his fingers, tearing away at her ribs.

The ax handle fell from her hand with a thump on the ground as she gripped the demon's wrist, trying to pry it away from her side, but he had hit her perfectly and she was in no position to overcome this blow.

With his free hand, the Boogerman grabbed her by the throat and lifted her off the ground, until her feet were dangling a good foot above the dirt. He squeezed her throat and she could feel the bones in her neck were dangerously close to crushing. She tried to pry his fingers away from her neck, but it was no use.

She was about to die and she knew it.

As she was about to lose consciousness for the last time in her life, she saw a fleeting movement out the corner of her eye. It was large and dark and there were two red flashes. She figured she was just seeing colors in her mind before she died.

Then she was released and knocked to the ground hard. As she went down, her head slammed against a rock and she became quite familiar with those times, when in the cartoons, a character gets conked in the head and starts seeing little birdies and stars circling their heads.

She fought to keep herself awake and found she could now breathe, but she could also feel the blood spitting out of her side with every breath.

She rolled onto her side and looked into the darkness and saw Bosley had the Boogerman down and had his jaws locked onto the demon's throat.

"Kill him, Bosley!" she croaked softly, not able to make much of a sound through her nearly crushed windpipe.

The Boogerman fought back and slashed at the hell hound, getting in a few good licks, causing Bosley to lose his grip on the demon. The Boogerman scrambled up and turned and took the fight straight at the hell hound, proving he was every bit as powerful as any of the Devil's dogs.

Bosley charged, knowing that this was the demon that had taken his master and his sister from him and he was ready to feast on his insides. As he closed on the demon, he got caught with another swing of the demon's fist and was knocked senseless.

The Boogerman looked down at the hell hound that was struggling to regain his feet and he roared.

"I ripped your sister's legs off and I'm going to do the same to you!"

He bent down to grab Bosley and Debbie could feel the tears beginning to well up in her eyes. She didn't want to see her friend dismembered like that and she fought to get up off the ground. But, her injuries were too much and she fell down again.

Just as the Boogerman reached down to grab Bosley, he was interrupted by another growl, one that he had never heard before.

Turning slowly, he found himself face-to-face with the biggest demon dog he had ever seen and those red eyes, way back inside that dark hood, flew open in wide terror.

He held out his right hand, trying to keep the demon dog back and Buster just clamped down on it with all the force of Hell. He didn't shake the

Boogerman or chomp on him or anything like that. He just growled at the demon, through his clenched teeth, letting him know that he wasn't scared of him and that he was a little more than miffed at how he was hurting his friends.

Buster pushed him backward with the arm that was still in his mouth and pressed him up against the side of the barn.

Debbie was still trying to fight off the fog clouding her mind when Cindy came running up to her and dropped down behind her.

"What are you doing here?" she croaked at her friend.

"How about a little thank you for showing your friends where you were?" said the young mother.

Bosley had finally gotten back up and was quickly back to his usual fighting self and he slowly walked over to the demon, who was still pinned against the barn wall.

Cindy helped Debbie up and started moving her away from what was about to become a very bloody battle. When they reached the edge of the clearing, Debbie's strength gave out and she fell to the ground and Cindy sat down behind her and cradled her in her arms.

"You really need to get out of here." said the deputy softly.

"I'm not going anywhere, girlfriend. If you're not

leaving, I'm not leaving."

They were about thirty yards away from the demon and the two hounds and Debbie just wanted to relax and watch and see what was going to happen.

Then from out of nowhere, they were joined by the sheriff, Tom, Cal and Agent Smith. The four men dropped down and began checking the two women out.

Brushing past all of them, Buttercup walked across the clearing. Nobody really paid much attention to him.

"Are you hurt?" asked her dad.

"Nothing a few days in the hospital won't fix," she said in a very raspy voice.

"We need to get you both out of here then," said Agent Smith.

"I'm not going anywhere!" coughed Debbie.

"Debbie, you're hurt," said Tom.

"I'm … not … leaving!" she said, this time pointing at the side of the barn.

It was then the four men noticed the two demon hounds and the Boogerman. The Boogerman was completely immobilized against the wall of the barn and the two hounds were just looking at him, wondering who was going to get the biggest piece of him.

Then a large, Bengal tiger moved in between the two dogs, making three sets of demon eyes looking at the Boogerman. Buttercup growled and so did Bosley. Buster tried to, but he still had the demon's arm halfway down his throat.

"Just sit down and enjoy the show," wheezed Debbie.

She felt Cindy's arms wrap around her and she just laid back against her friend, feeling safer right then that she had for the last month.

Then, it was almost as if a movie director had yelled, "Action!"

The demon began fighting for his life. He brought his free fist crashing down on Buster's head and it drove the demon dog to his knees. But it wasn't enough to be released from his grip.

Bosley lunged at the Boogerman, going for the free arm and the demon swung and connected with the side of the hell hound's head, knocking him completely around.

Buttercup lunged in and grabbed the demon's other arm and held it firmly between his jaws.

In a massive show of strength, the Boogerman brought his arms together in front of himself and slammed Buster and Buttercup's heads together. Both released their holds as they tried to figure out what had happened.

When the sheriff saw how the fight was going, he flipped the switch on his rifle and Debbie could hear it powering up.

"Don't you fire unless it's a last resort," she said, looking up at her father. "You let them handle him."

John just looked down at her and then nodded.

The Boogerman came away from the barn wall, knocking Buster backward a couple of steps and then smashed his fist into the top of Buster's head again. This drove Buster down onto his font knees.

When the demon found himself free again, he turned to flee and was immediately grabbed around the ankle by Bosley, who left no doubts that he intended to tear that leg off the demon. What was good enough for his sister, was good enough for this demon.

The Boogerman swung his fist again and almost brained the hell hound, but Bosley had decided that he was never going to let go of this demon again. When this night was over, he was going to have demon leg to chew on.

The demon went to hit Bosley again, but never got the chance. Buster grabbed hold of one arm and Buttercup got hold of the other. They started pulling him backward, away from Bosley.

Of course, Bosley still had a firm grip on the demon's leg and he was getting dragged along with him. He started wrenching the demon's leg back and forth and the demon screeched in pain.

"Tear him apart!" croaked Debbie.

As if the hounds and tiger heard her, they

decided to follow her orders. Bosley yanked even harder on the leg and the other two kept pulling on his arms. With one last pull, the demon's leg separated from his body, bringing the loudest scream of pain any living being had ever heard.

Bosley shook his head back and forth and let go of the leg, flinging it across the clearing, where it landed right at the feet of Agent Smith, who promptly doubled over and threw up.

Bosley lunged again and this time got hold of the demon's other leg. He and Buster and Buttercup started pulling in opposite directions and this time it was Buttercup rewarded with a new chew toy.

Everyone could hear the arm coming loose from the demon's body and it sent cold shivers of disgust through all their bodies. There is quite a nasty sound made by a body being ripped to pieces right in front of your eyes.

Debbie felt a wave of sorrow float across her mind, feeling sorry for a moment that Kenny Kline was suffering like that, but she banished that thought immediately. He didn't deserve any pity.

The Boogerman was flailing about, not really fighting anymore. He'd already lost an arm and a leg, so he didn't have much to fight with anymore. His body was going into the death throes spasms.

He was still able to scream in pain and Buster decided he had heard enough. He clamped down on the demon's head and everyone heard a muffled screech as Buster ripped his head from the body.

Then, the giant demon dog made everyone sick, by chomping a few times on the head and then swallowing it. He looked around at the others. Bosley was looking at him like he was some kind of hero. If Bosley could have spoken, he would have said something like, "I love you, man."

Debbie looked at Buster and said, "You know, that's going to make you sick when you get small again."

Buster walked over to her and the others and lowered his head to them.

Woof.

He went to lick Debbie's face, but she put her hand up and pushed him back.

"Ewww, you just ate a demon head. I don't want your kiss. Not until you brush your teeth."

Woof.

They all looked up at Bosley, who was rubbing up against his buddy.

John looked at them and said, "Oh, you two are buddies now, huh."

Woof.

John and Cindy helped Debbie to her feet and then were surprised to hear the sound of a weapon discharging. They looked toward the barn to see Agent Smith, firing his weapon into the body of the demon, over and over again.

After about a dozen shots, he walked back to the group.

Cal asked him, "Is he dead now?"

Smith looked at him and said, "I'm just making sure he never comes back."

Cal held his hand out and Smith took it.

"Martin, you're a good man."

John walked over to the remains of the body and pulled a canister from his belt, He twisted a dial on the top and then set it down into one of the holes that Smith had blasted in the body and turned and walked away.

"Shall we go?" he asked. "We need to get Debbie to the hospital. Again."

As they turned to walk away, the canister ignited and set the remains of the body on fire with a white, hot flame.

Then Cindy looked around and said, "Bosley, NO!"

Everyone looked at the hell hound and started laughing. He had the leg he had torn off the demon, firmly in his mouth.

Cal reached out and took the leg from the hell hound's mouth and said, "Give me that."

He took the leg over to the burning body and dropped it on the flames and then looked around and found the dismembered arm and did the same thing with it.

Then the nine of them turned and headed back down the mountain. Buster, Bosley and Buttercup took up the lead, walking side-by-side like best buddies.

Cindy was finally able to smile and enjoy the company of her friend, knowing that the nightmare was over.

There was laughing, joking and the occasional gasp of pain from Debbie.

She was just happy to still be alive to feel it.

Chapter 19
~~
Another day in Monster Town

Jake and Randy were sitting in their beds and looked up to see Debbie standing in the doorway to their semi-private hospital room.

"So, are you boys ready to head home?"

"Absolutely," said Jake.

"If for no other reason than to get away from that evil witch out there at the nurse's station," said Randy.

"Kelly? She's about the sweetest nurse I've ever met," laughed Debbie.

Farmer Smith appeared at the door behind Debbie. He was walking with crutches and had Kelly walking alongside, helping him.

"You boys are a couple of wusses. You'll go fight the Boogerman, but you can't handle your sweet, little sister?"

Jake looked at the three of them and shook his head. Then he looked at his brother.

"Bro, we need to get the hell out of here. We're outnumbered."

"Well, you two hurry up and get out of here," said Debbie. "I have to go. I promised to give a couple of friends a ride."

She turned and headed out of the hospital, still walking a little slow from all the bandages she had wrapped around her midsection. The Boogerman had done a bit of damage, but there was no way in hell she was going to stay in that hospital for one more minute.

She went and climbed up into the truck. But, it wasn't her truck. It was a big flat-bed tow truck. She looked over at Earl behind the wheel.

"Ready to go, little lady?"

"Absolutely and thank you for doing this."

"No problem."

They turned and headed west on the main drag and turned into the driveway just short of the bridge over the creek. Pulling back to the barn near the back of the property, they saw Kyle waving at them.

"C'mon in guys," he said as they climbed out of the truck.

As the three of them walked into the barn, they found Bosley laying on a pile of straw and he had a little wiener dog curled up next to him. The little dog looked like he was having a bad day.

"I don't know what he got into last night, but he must have eaten something that doesn't agree with him. He's been like this all morning, laying around, moaning and whimpering."

Debbie looked at Kyle and smiled, "I'm sure it's nothing Kyle. I'll bet it will pass in no time."

"Well, I hope so. Anyway, I don't think it would be right to separate these two now. What do you think of taking Buster along with Bosley? They are best friends now."

"You sure about that?" asked Debbie.

"Deputy, I came out here last night and found both of them gone. Buster's cage was wide open and it looks like he has figured out how to open it. If I can't keep him contained, well, you know what your poppa said."

Debbie looked at the two dogs and noticed a very guilty look on Bosley's face.

"Sure, we can take both of them. You know where they'll be, so you can go visit both of them anytime."

Kyle nodded as Debbie looked at the two dogs again.

"You two ready to go for a ride?"

Bosley jumped up and was ready to head for the door. Buster staggered to get himself up on his feet and Debbie reached down and picked him up, cradling him in her arms.

As they walked out of the barn, Debbie leaned down and whispered into Buster's ear, "I told you that eating that demon head was going to come back and haunt you."

Buster just whimpered and laid his head down on her arm.

Earl got Bosley up on the back of the truck and

clipped his chain into the winch hook. The hell hound just laid down and got comfortable.

Debbie climbed into the truck and had Buster on her lap as Kyle reached in and scratched his head.

"I'll come by and see you in a couple of days, buddy."

Buster licked his hand as Earl started the truck. As they turned around and started back to the front of the property, Debbie turned and called out through the sliding window behind her head.

"Bosley."

The hell hound stood up and poked his nose through the window.

"Did you open Buster's cage?"

Woof.

She laughed and reached up and ran her hand over his nose.

"Thanks, buddy."

She turned back and watched as they rolled through town. People were out walking around, enjoying being out in the sunshine and not living in the fear they had known for the past month.

She ran her hand over Buster's belly and could feel it was a bit bulged out in the middle. She felt a little sorry for the demon dog, but she knew he'd be feeling much better in a few days after it passed.

Pulling into a farm with a large steel building, she could feel Bosley looking over her shoulder and panting and whining.

She got out and Buster wiggled around, letting her know he wanted down. She set him down and let him walk on his own. Earl unclipped the chain holding the hell hound and Bosley was so excited he couldn't contain himself. He was shaking so hard with anticipation, Debbie was afraid he was going to shake himself to pieces.

As they walked up to the building, the door opened and out rolled a big guy in a wheelchair.

"Hey Bill. I thought it was time to bring him home."

Bill looked up at Bosley, who was jumping and leaping all around him, yipping with excitement. He laughed at the sight of his hell hound acting like a little kid.

"Hey buddy, did you miss me?"

Bosley nuzzled his wet nose into the side of Bill's face and slobbered all over him.

"Ewww, you better settle down or I'll feed you to Buster. I swear to God I will!"

Debbie started laughing and Bill looked at her.

"I don't think that threat is going to fly anymore, Bill."

Just then Buster ran between her legs and jumped his front paws up on Bill's knees.

"What's this?" asked the werewolf.

"It has been decided that these two couldn't be

separated now. Besides, Buster is becoming more than the Manning's can handle. We figured he wouldn't be any trouble for you."

"Good grief."

"Hey Bosley, is Buster your best buddy now?"

Bosley jumped up and howled loud and long. Buster yipped and then tried to howl.

"How am I supposed to control him now?"

"Don't know, Bill. Maybe be friends with the two of them, I guess," said Earl.

Bill reached up and ran his hand over Bosley's ear and scratched it.

"So, how long do you think you'll be in this chair?" asked Debbie.

"Doc says I should be up and around in a few weeks. Probably about the time of the next full moon."

"Well, hurry it up. The town needs you and Bosley working again."

"Hopefully not for a long time."

"True. Okay, we need to get going. They're your problem now."

She reached up and kissed Bosley on the cheek and patted him on the neck.

"Thank you, buddy, for keeping me and Cindy alive."

She did the same thing to Buster, who just wagged his tail furiously.

"They did great, did they?"

"They both did great, along with Buttercup. Take care, Bill."

They turned and walked back to the truck as Bill turned his chair around and said, "C'mon you two, inside and you can tell me all about how you guys took down the Boogerman."

Bosley and Buster bounded through the open door and there was a loud crash almost immediately.

"Bosley! I swear you are going to become somebody's food!"

Debbie and Earl laughed as they climbed into the truck.

~~~~

Debbie walked into the department and it was a full house. It wouldn't have been nearly as crowded except for the presence of a full grown, Bengal tiger.

Buttercup was laying on the floor with his head resting in Agent Smith's lap. Smith was stroking his fur and Debbie could swear she heard the tiger purring.

"I see you've found a new friend," she said to Smith.

"Well, he kind of grows on a person."

Cal was leaning up against a file cabinet and Dean was sitting in a chair across from her father. He was just as bandaged up as Debbie, but he also was not going to spend another minute in that hospital.

Mabel was at her desk, filling in some paperwork.

Dean stood up and said, "Well, he needs to ungrow because it's time to head home. The missus is going to start wondering what the heck I'm doing down here. Let's go, buddy."

Buttercup cracked one eye open and then slowly climbed to his feet. In just a few seconds he shrank back down to a regular sized cat and jumped onto John's desk and then onto Dean's shoulder.

"Ladies, gentlemen, take care."

"Dean, thanks for coming down," said John.

"You betcha."

Then he turned and headed out the door.

Cal sat down in the empty chair and looked at Smith.

"Well, Martin. What do you think of your time here in Monster Town?"

The fed looked at him and said, "I think I'll head back to DC and sit at a desk for a little while."

"We could probably find a position here for you," said John.

"No thank you, sheriff. You people have to deal with a lot more than I think I'm capable of."

"Okay, but the offer is always available. Just remember one thing."

"What's that?"

John looked at Debbie, Cal and Mabel and all three of them said the same thing.

"There's no such thing as monsters!"

Smith laughed, "Monsters? Never heard of 'em"

He stood up and John and Cal did, too. They each shook his hand as he was heading for the door. He turned and looked at Debbie and said, "Good working with you, deputy."

"Same here. Just make sure to keep that safety set on your weapon."

Smith laughed and turned and walked out the door.

~~~~

Later that evening, as the sun had just gone down, Debbie sat on her front porch, rocking back and forth. Raising the glass of lemonade to her lips, she savored the sweet, tangy taste.

"How come you never told the others who the Boogerman really was?"

She looked at her friend sitting next to her and smiled.

"Sweetie, after all the pain he put you through, he doesn't deserve to be remembered. If you don't tell anyone who he was, he will be forgotten in time."

Cindy looked at her and said, "I'll never tell. I'm just glad that my nightmares can finally be over."

They looked out into the yard and watched as Toby chased some fireflies.

"So, you never did tell me why you're not one hundred percent human."

Debbie sat back and took a deep breath and laughed.

"Well sweetie, let's just say my mom is from out of town."

"Really?" asked Cindy. "Like, from where?"

"From way out of town. Like, many light years out of town."

"Ohhhh."

The End …

I hope you've enjoyed this story about Debbie, John and the hounds. And all the others. These Cold Shivers Nightmares are meant to be stand-alone novels, but that doesn't mean that there won't be more stories with Deputy Dinkie … err … I mean, Deputy Debbie.

I would appreciate it if you could visit the website of your favorite bookseller and leave a review. Obviously I would love to get 4 and 5 star ratings, but more than that, I'd like to get honest ratings so I can see how these stories are being received. Thank you for taking the time to read my stories.

Be sure to check out the next book in the series.

Shattered Prisons

When things go bump in the night, maybe you should just sell the house and move.

For the last few months before her death, artist Julie's beloved Nana started to talk about strange things - evil demons, dark angels and bad humans. Julie let her prattle - it was just harmless talk, wasn't it? Wasn't it?

Now on her own with her grief in a big empty house, Julie's beginning to think that maybe there was something to Nana's wild talk. Most normal families have skeletons in the closet. Julie's family is a little more unusual ... her closet has demons.

Demons are on the loose, a friend is in peril, and a family legacy has been thrust upon her surprised shoulders. Can Julie transform into a badass demon fighting machine or will she cower behind her easel?

With the forces of evil on the prowl - released from their prisons by a clumsy friend - Julie must scramble to train and take her place beside Templar Knights, demon-fighting monks and a feisty Dominican nun who has an obsession with cherry pie.

Paranormal horror with a touch of humor and dose of hair-raising shivers, this is the perfect novel for the Goosebumps kid who has outgrown Goosebumps.

Also Available

**Into The Wishing Well
by D Glenn Casey**

Melanie Peters was a good girl, always doing what she felt was right. She had a good life, even looking forward to her wedding in a few months. But then, an "accident" sent her to the Pearly Gates before her time. Not only did they tell her she was not expected, but they couldn't let her in at that time.

So, what's a girl to do?

Wicked Rising
The Chronicles of Wyndweir
Book One

by D Glenn Casey

Garlan has finished his trials in the Land of the Dragons and he is heading home. The only thing he can think of is being reunited with the woman that has stolen his heart.

But, there is evil rising in the Eastern Desert and war is on the horizon. Everyone he knows is expecting him to rise up and be a leader and vanquish this evil. He'd rather they find someone else.

The Tales of Garlan
by D Glenn Casey

Garlan went to live with the old wizard, Sigarick when he was eight years old. Now, in his twenty-third year it's time to prove he's actually learned something.

These four short stories tell of wizard duel, clearing thugs from villages and facing a final set of trials that could very well kill him. All in a days work for Garlan.

Printed in Great Britain
by Amazon